PRAISE FOR *CARAVAN STORY*

'Wayne Macauley's first novel, *Blueprints for a
Barbed-Wire Canoe*, showed that a real talent had
arrived and his second confirms the promise.'
Age

'Mixing elegy and whimsy, satire
and black humour, language becomes
pliant under Macauley's command.'
Australian Book Review

'Part satire, part Orwellian fable,
Caravan Story is compulsively readable.'
The Monthly

Wayne Macauley has published three novels, most recently
The Cook, and the short fiction collection *Other Stories*.
He lives in Melbourne.
waynemacauley.com

CARAVAN
STORY

WAYNE MACAULEY

TEXT PUBLISHING MELBOURNE AUSTRALIA

textpublishing.com.au

The Text Publishing Company
Swann House
22 William Street
Melbourne Victoria 3000
Australia

First published by Black Pepper, Melbourne Australia, 2007
This edition published by The Text Publishing Company, 2012

Cover design by WH Chong
Page design by Text
Printed and bound in Australia by Griffin Press

Epigraph from *The Harz Journey* by Heinrich Heine, translated by Frederic T. Wood and adapted by Robert C. Holub and Martha Humphreys. Published in *Heinrich Heine: Poetry and Prose*, Continuum, New York, 1982.

Some of the ideas in Pt. II, Ch. 2 of *Caravan Story* were drawn from Syd Field's *Screenplay*, published by Dell Publishing, New York, 1984.

National Library of Australia Cataloguing-in-Publication entry:
Author: Macauley, Wayne.
Title: Caravan story / Wayne Macauley.
ISBN: 9781922079121 (pbk.)
ISBN: 9781921961359 (ebook : epub)
Subjects: Trailer camps—Fiction.
Dewey Number: A823.3

The paper this book is printed on is certified against the Forest Stewardship Council® Standards. Griffin Press holds FSC chain of custody certification SGS-COC-005088. FSC promotes environmentally responsible, socially beneficial and economically viable management of the world's forests.

For D

...I no longer know where irony ceases and heaven begins...

Heinrich Heine, *The Harz Journey*

PART ONE

one

It is seven o'clock, I just heard the click as the clock hit the hour, and the bulldozer has started up outside. We're both in bed, her leg curled over my thigh, her warm breath on my neck. We woke early, around six, smiled a sad smile then rolled over and slept again. The noise alone is already shaking the windows, the glass of water beside the clock is vibrating gently. They'll start with the laundry, then take the bathroom, so we'd best make our way there now.

I stand on the edge of the toilet seat while she pisses and look out through the louvres onto the backyard. They must still be warming up the bulldozer and having their smoke in the driveway down the side because the backyard is deserted, bathed in morning sunlight. The only tree, a plum, is showing its first blossom and a wave of genuine sadness passes over me when I realise it will be the first thing to go. She kicks me off the toilet seat and stands up on tiptoe to look herself. I piss in the basin. The plum tree, she says. Yes, I say, and turn on the tap. We climb back into bed just as the bulldozer revs and moves and a shuddering sound can be heard as it turns from the driveway into the backyard, taking the plum tree in its path, backing up, revving, then moving forward again, manoeuvring the laundry into its sights.

We lie in bed on our backs, I put my hands behind my head and she nestles her head in the crook of my elbow. We lie like that for a long time, lost in our own thoughts, then I get up again to make tea and toast. Why not? I say, when she looks at me strangely.

Cracks have already appeared in the kitchen and the stove is covered with a thin layer of white dust. The bull-dozer passes back and forth close to the kitchen window. I can see the driver from the chest down, his left foot working the clutch. A voice shouts instructions—Back a bit! Forward!—and I can hear the timber and plaster cracking and breaking. I stand at the kitchen sink waiting for the kettle to boil and watch the big black wheel pass before me, so close that I can see the scars in the rubber and tiny bits of debris embedded in the tread. The kettle doesn't boil; I check the switch, put my hands around it. I turn on the light switch but there is no light. I go back

4

to the bedroom and tell her—she's half asleep and doesn't really understand—then go out the back door and pick up some pieces of wood. A man leans on a shovel—why a shovel?—and I nod to him. He just stares, doesn't know what to say, then disappears around the corner where the bulldozer is working. I bring the old heat-bead barbecue back in from the shed, set it up in the kitchen, arrange some paper and wood and light a fire. When the flames have died down I toast some bread on a carving fork and soon have a saucepan of water boiled. She smiles, having smelled the smoke, then laughs, seeing the blackened toast; we laugh together, so loud that we can no longer hear the dozer or the cracking of timber in the kitchen. We eat our toast and drink our cups of tea.

It's going to be hot. The sun is already on the window and we can feel the new day's warmth seeping through the blanket into the room. On these days we'd already be up, drinking our tea in the backyard in the sun. The planes flying in to land at the airport are shedding silver from their wings as they bank towards the runway. Next door's cat is stretched out on the warm concrete, purring lightly with every breath. The first cigarette is hot and bitter, the smoke hanging in thin clouds above our heads, and the light already so intense that you have to squint to form a shape: the shed, the back fence, the neighbours' roof.

These are the days when we are happy, thankful for what we have. Small black ants march purposefully beneath us, sweet air drifts to us from the jasmine on the shed.

A man is standing in the bedroom doorway. For some reason I think it's her father, though her father looks nothing like that, then perhaps the lawyer I'd jokingly said we should ask for, then a workman, which it is. He looks so awkward and fidgety that I almost invite him to bed. He stands there fidgeting for some time. She's not conscious of him so it doesn't matter, she's dozing again; it's obvious he wants to speak but something very firm and persistent has got his tongue. I explain the situation to him as clearly as possible: the house was unoccupied, we've lived here undisturbed for over three years, we've painted the hallway and the two front rooms, fixed up the front garden, kept the lawn down, replaced three windows, cleaned out the back shed, pruned the plum tree, made a vegetable patch, planted a passionfruit vine along the back fence. He's lit a cigarette and I realise he's not looking at me any more and probably not listening either. He's looking at her. I look at her too; the blanket has slipped down just enough to reveal a breast and a nipple. It's the strangest thing then, for a minute or so, as he looks from his angle and I from mine at the shoulder, the flank, the breast and the nipple, her hair on the pillow, a streak of morning light on the wall beside her head. The bulldozer starts up—I hadn't noticed the silence—and the moment is broken. I look at the clock—quarter past ten. That was smoko—he turns from the doorway and goes back to work. I sit there looking, first at the empty doorway, then at her flesh. It's all going to pieces, I say to myself: I know what I mean and I don't feel false at all.

I make love to her quietly. She hardly wakes, neither at the sound of my soft moaning nor the shuddering outside. I kiss the nipple that the man has seen but it's no longer mine, it moves away from me, sinks softly into her breast at my lips' touch and doesn't rise again. She's getting old, I think—how old?—within what seems like an instant her flesh has lost its spring. She rolls away from me, perhaps sensing my thoughts, and I roll away from her. The clock is bouncing on the bedside table and the glass of water is gone. Nothing lasts, nothing lasts; neither this nor anything that comes after. Days dance on a pinhead, months fly up to the moon; already the laundry's gone. We lie back to back for a very long time.

I must be dozing, daydreaming, because now we're somewhere else. She's wearing her old cotton dress with the hole under the arm, I've pulled on a pair of jeans and am carrying a t-shirt. A park opens up before us, a park

I remember from long ago: we sit by the pond and throw crusts to the ducks. One comes up close and almost pecks her bare foot; she grabs me tight and buries her head in my chest and I laugh. We can still hear the noise of the bulldozer though it now sounds more like a plane flying low overhead and all of a sudden we're surrounded by a cluster of gnats. She tells me they're attracted to the heat of our bodies, that she heard this on the radio and that it's all perfectly true, so we wade out into the pond until we are up to our necks and stay there like that kissing for a while until the gnats have gone. Then we're dozing again, I mean dozing inside the dream, because for a long time all I know is that our eyes are closed and nothing at all is happening and when I open my eyes she has just opened hers too and I say: Were you dozing? And she says: Yes, I just opened my eyes then. We laugh, and the dream is broken, the dream or the memory, I'm still not sure, and a veil of white plaster dust has covered our lids.

You'll have to go now, says a voice. It's the workman again. I push her gently, whisper in her ear: We have to go. It's already afternoon. Out the front they have a caravan waiting for us, fixed to the back of a four-wheel drive. A woman is standing with the door open, a clipboard tucked under her arm. She's very well dressed, her hair is shiny and she gives off a faint scent of green apples. All the neighbours are standing around, restraining their children and dogs; I smile at them as we walk towards the van. Please don't move around too much inside, the woman says, and she closes the door behind us.

It's not a particularly new caravan, nor is it particularly clean. I run a finger across the fold-down table and pick up a smudge of black grime. We sit ourselves down opposite each other at the table and the van begins to move; I pull back the curtains a little with my hand and look out; the neighbours are now standing on the footpath in a line, watching us go. My partner reaches into the cupboard above us and finds a can of tuna, I reach into the drawer beside me and take out a can opener and two forks. We eat the tuna, spearing a small chunk each with our forks, first she, then me, in turns, like a tea party; occasionally the tin slides across the table, first towards her, then towards me; we push it back into the middle each time and smile. The tuna lasts a while, there's nothing else to do, neither of us wants to get up and move about because of the woman's instructions. We're very tired, but nor do we want to sleep; we're both very anxious in a way to see what happens next.

We travel for some time; through the parted curtains I see factories, car yards, paddocks of dead grass, all bathed in rusty twilight. Huge steel pylons march away to the horizon, the powerlines slung between them. On and on, on and on. She looks out her side, I look out mine. I close my eyes and remember the story of a ride in a troika through the vast Russian wastes; thatched huts outside the window, the driver's greatcoat dusted with snow, the horses' heads tossing, white breath from their nostrils. I spend some time remembering this story in all its detail before opening my eyes again. The caravan has stopped. Everything is quiet. The woman opens the door. Sleep now, she says, and she closes the door again. We hear a clunk as the caravan is unhooked from the towbar; I part the curtains and peer outside but everything is dark. We let down the table and make up a bed but neither of us can sleep.

I hear voices outside and go to the window at the far end of the van. I can just make out a toilet block with a flickering fluorescent light and people going in and coming out with towels slung over their shoulders. We're in a caravan park, I say. She joins me at the window and we watch the people coming and going from the toilet block and the woman with the folder scurrying here and there. Will they let us have a shower? she says. I doubt it, I say. We close the curtains again and lie in bed. Take off your top, I say. She does. I cup one breast in my hand and gaze at the nipple. It's all going to pieces, I say, then say it again. But her eyes are closed, she doesn't or doesn't want to hear or hears but doesn't want to answer and I pull the blanket up over her to the neck and sit on the edge of the bed with my head in my hands listening to the murmuring voices outside. This is our new life, she says, it's all beginning again. I feel very close to her then but instead of speaking or touching her I remain on the edge of the bed and say nothing. A new life, I think, she's probably right. Very probably, very probably. She puts a hand on the small of my back.

Then there's a clunk and the caravan shakes—we're being hooked up again. She sits up in bed, I look out the window; cars are starting up and headlights are coming on. The first van pulls away and the others follow. I go to the front window. A different car is towing us now, an early model sedan. The van jerks and moves, I hurry back to the other window, steadying myself on the stove, the sink, and cheek to cheek we look out at the convoy moving off into the night.

We watch the dark, our heads start to loll, our eyelids droop, it's been a big day, cheek to cheek the murmur of the road lulls us into sleep. I don't dream, I don't think she dreams either; when the morning light through the curtains wakes us we find we've slept top to tail. I stare at her toes and stroke the curve of her arch. We're still on the road, occasionally we feel a bump and shudder, at other times a gentle swaying from side to side. It's very beautiful inside the caravan, the glow at the window and the seeping warmth, the gentle swaying, the hum of the road. If this is our new home then I'm happy with it, happy for her, happy for me. From where I lie on my back I purse my lips, blow the curtain back a little away from the window and catch glimpses of blue cloudless sky. Yesterday is already a lifetime away, and the memory of it frayed: a bulldozer came, we slept in a while, then we got up, and the journey began. Brief shadows of branches overhanging the road flicker across my face; a warm draft from somewhere, perhaps under the door, caresses my half-open eyes.

I'm hungry, she says. She's sitting up. I look at her framed by the window opposite, soft down around the rims of her ears. She's taken her hair and bunched it up into a mound on top of her head. I love her too much to say anything; she reads my eyes and smiles. There might be more tuna, I say. She screws up her face. Perhaps we should wait till we've stopped. We might never stop, she says, and she gets out of bed. The idea hadn't occurred to me and I lie there wondering about it for a while. She looks through the cupboards, the small gas fridge, on the shelves and under the beds. We'll starve, she says. She crawls over me and looks out the back. Look, she says. I look too; behind us into the distance a convoy of caravans follows, between each caravan a cluster of cars, waiting for the chance to pass. We close the curtains again. To the slaughter, I think, not quite sure where the thought has come from: uncomplaining, like lambs to the slaughter.

Suddenly we're on a bumpy road, the curtains quiver, one cupboard handle rattles, through the side window we see a couple of houses flash past, one with a small boy standing at the gate. I pull on my pants, she fixes her skirt, a great feeling of excitement has now overtaken us. The caravan shakes, changes direction, then changes direction again; the surface beneath us is now hard corrugated ground, then gravel, a moment of asphalt, gravel again, we turn sharply, then something soft, perhaps grass. The caravan stops, we hear the door of the car in front slam, other cars pulling up behind. We each put a hand on the wall, trying to adjust ourselves to the sudden stillness. We've stopped, she says. Just then the door opens and the woman pokes her head inside. You can come out now, she says. Have we been hiding? I think. The woman's face disappears again.

We step down out of the caravan and look around. We're on a football oval, surrounded by paddocks; in the far distance I can see a farmhouse, in the foreground the footballers' brick changing shed. The caravans have formed a circle, like wagons arrayed against an attack. The drivers are all getting out of their vehicles and gathering over at the changing shed; some slip inside to use the toilets, the others form a close-knit group and start handing around their cigarettes. The woman strides around the circle, the clipboard under her arm, knocking on each caravan door and poking her head inside. The people start stepping out, dazed and confused like us: some old, some young, some with children who immediately start running around together madly on the grass.

Gather round, the woman says, gather round, don't be shy. She is standing in the centre of the oval on the concrete cricket pitch; she throws out an arm then brings it towards her, as if gathering air to her bosom. Gather round, she says, gather round. We all take a few steps forward. I can see a couple of the drivers chuckling, leaning on the boundary fence. Gather round, she says, as step by step the circle closes in. In an arc, she says, and we somehow manage to arrange ourselves in an arc. A little closer, she says, don't be shy—and as a group we shuffle forward.

We all stand shoulder to shoulder: behind the woman, beyond the fence, I can see the old timber scoreboard: 'H——' above and 'Visitors' below, painted in large white letters. H——, I whisper, but someone behind me says, Shh! The woman is talking, her name is Polly, she

appreciates our patience, we will be eating shortly, there
are showers in the changing shed, men to the left, women
to the right, this will be our home for a while. Are there
any questions? she asks. Someone asks are dogs allowed.
The woman smiles and answers yes. A young child breaks
away from the group and runs back to her caravan; the dog
is let out, it starts yapping and turning in circles. A small
ripple of laughter passes through the group. Is there a
phone we can use? someone asks. The woman says there's a
public phone in town, a driver can take us there after we've
eaten. The woman pauses, raises her eyebrows, passes her
eye across every face. We look at the ground, or at the sky;
no-one has any more questions.

We all move back to our caravans, to freshen up
before lunch. The drivers have lit a fire in a cut-down
diesel drum, they are standing around it, drinking cans
of beer; from behind the shed two of them carry out a
big steel grate and drop it on top of the drum. I think I
might have a shower, she says. There's a queue already, I
say. But she doesn't care, she'll wait, she says: if she doesn't
have a shower soon she'll die. She takes a towel from the
cupboard (*Towels and all, I think*) and walks back towards
the door. What do you think? I ask, as she puts her foot on
the step. She turns around and shrugs her shoulders. We'll
just have to wait and see, she says.

I pull the curtains open and watch the goings-on outside. The day is already hot and shade here hard to come by. People are moving to and from the changing shed with towels slung over their shoulders. I see her stop and talk to someone—a young woman about the same age—and they enter the right-hand end of the shed together. For a while I keep looking at the shed, and the dark doorway they have disappeared into. But then for some reason I can't look any longer and I pull the curtains closed again.

I haven't eaten since the tuna—that seems like days ago now—and as I lie on my back on the bed again my stomach starts to rumble. I lay one hand across it and the other hand across my chest. I'm trying to calm myself down, though I don't feel upset at all. All day I've felt this calm, this I-don't-care-we'll-see-what-happens-it-doesn't-matter kind of calm. I can't get excited about anything, or get upset about anything either. As if to test myself I move the hand that was on my stomach down towards my crotch but then my stomach rumbles again.

She comes back freshly showered, a strand of wet hair stuck to her cheek. She sits on the bottom bunk at the far end of the caravan, lays the towel over her head, twists it into a turban and throws her head back. Only then does she look at me, seeing what I think. I let it go; I don't think anything. I'm looking out the window again;

they are carrying a large wooden trestle table out into the centre of the oval. Polly follows, a cask of wine in each hand. People start appearing at the doors of their caravans. Polly flutters around, encouraging them to take a plate and form a queue at the barbecue. Formlessly at first, they do. Are you hungry? I ask. She's drying her hair now, like out of a painting or a movie, her legs spread wide, her head between them, her hair falling down, rubbing her scalp with the towel.

We go out together, it's a long time since we've been out, and though I know as I think it that it is a ridiculous thought, I think: At least we're going out. From the trestle table beside the players' gate you take a paper plate, move forward to the barbecue where you choose your meat, then back around to the other gate where you help yourself to the salads. We choose a quiet place at the row of tables in the centre of the oval but soon we are joined by others. To her left sits an energetic-looking man with greying hair, probably in his early forties. To my right sits a young couple, both dressed in baggy clothes and smelling of sandalwood. The young man leans past the young woman towards me and says: All that's missing is the string quartet! He lets out a giggle and returns to his plate.

Meanwhile my partner has struck up a conversation with her neighbour. I catch only bits of it—our table is full now, the other tables too, and a lively hubbub of talk has begun. It seems he's an actor, they're comparing shows they've seen, in particular something from years ago in which, they now realise, they both had a mutual friend. She leans back to introduce me to him: This is Wayne, she says: this is Andrew. Hi Andrew, I say. Wayne's a writer, she says. Andrew nods and smiles. She leans forward and they continue talking.

I have chosen the chicken wings but they are not cooked in the middle. Around the joint the flesh is pink and streaked with blood. I look around the table, everyone is eating theirs. My eye falls on Polly. Unfortunately, just as I look at her, she looks at me. There's something strange about her look, something that actually frightens me—I don't know why or what it is exactly but I know in that moment that I must take what I'm given and, in a practical sense, I must eat the chicken wings without complaint, no matter how badly cooked. I pick up the bone from my plate again and sink my teeth into the uncooked flesh. Polly goes back to her meal.

A strange thought starts moving through me. We are eating our last meal, I think, and will soon be coaxed into the changing shed perhaps under the pretext of an after-dinner dance where the doors will be locked and bolted and the gas taps turned up full. They'll get a big bulldozer to dig a big pit, dump us in and cover us over. On top of us they'll build a shopping centre or a sporting complex or perhaps new municipal offices. For a while those who knew us will try to track us down but they will soon be put off the scent. It won't take long for us all to be forgotten—this too has been thought out in advance. In thinking all this I've managed to amuse myself and am now looking down at the plate of scraps in front of me, smiling. But then the young woman beside me starts nudging my arm with her elbow and thrusts a long tube of white plastic cups in my face. I take one and pass it on. Two casks of wine follow: one white, one red. I take the white and fill my cup. Now Polly is up, tapping her plastic cup with a fork, a gesture that provokes some good-natured laughter from the crowd. Polly responds. Yes, she says, yes of course, she says, no long-stemmed crystal here. But if I could just have your attention for a moment, please, there are a few things I want to say. Everyone goes silent and gives Polly their attention. Even the drivers, still gathered around the barbecue, turn and look in her direction and respect-fully lower their cans. You have all been very patient, says Polly, and I would like to thank you for that. The problem was that the salads had been left back in Melbourne and the shop here had no lettuce. Eventually you will be allowed to cook in your caravans but the arrangements for that are still pending. A watch has been found in the showers—Polly holds up the watch. A woman stands up, embarrassed, and the watch is handed down the table to her. Polly adjusts the neck of her dress. A few more things, she says.

The children are getting restless, one of them has crawled under the table and her mother is whispering angrily at her to get back in her chair. The heat has become unbearable, and that combined with the wine has put blank stupefied looks on everyone's faces. But Polly is talking again. She talks for a long time, but I understand very little of what she says. It's as if her words are now being spoken in a room at the far end of a corridor, I'm too tired to strain my ear, something soft and dull inside my head keeps distracting me. I don't think the others understand much either. Everyone is trying their best, they're looking at her and listening, but they just don't understand. She finishes and asks do we have any questions. I put up my hand to speak. Is there something we can clean the caravan with, I say, some cleaning liquid or something? Polly smiles. Come around to the car after lunch, she says. I have stood up to ask the question, without realising that I have, and though I'm satisfied with the answer I feel awkward when I sit back down. I pick up my plastic cup and self-consciously drink the drop that's left.

When I go to Polly's car after lunch Polly is not there. I see her hurrying towards me. She's had a huge day, it's all fallen on her shoulders, she's wearing a sleeveless purple cotton dress and I can see the sweat glistening in the creases under her arms and the dark crescent moon stains beneath. She apologises for being late, someone went missing, but they've found them now. I almost want to hug her, tell her to calm down. She opens the back of the four-wheel drive and begins pulling the boxes towards her, opening the flaps on the top, then pushing them away again. She finally finds the one she wants. She takes out a bottle of Lemon Jif and a three-pack of Chux Superwipes. What's all this about? I ask. Polly looks at me, the cleaning items still in her hand. I just explained it all at lunch, she says. I say I didn't understand and I don't think the others did either. Polly pushes the Jif and the Superwipes into my hands and closes the door again. I'd advise you not to ask too many questions, she says. She looks me straight in the eye: I'd think yourself lucky if I were you; a lot of people have been working very hard, myself included, to set this up, and I'd appreciate your cooperation. What's your name? she says. Wayne, I answer, Wayne Macauley. All right, Wayne, she says, now go and clean up your van.

It's so hot in there when I get back that I have to open all the windows. My partner hasn't come back from lunch;

she must be talking to the actor she met. The inspiration to clean has now completely deserted me, it's too hot to do anything. I lie on the bottom bunk and count the wooden slats of the bed above. I can still smell Polly's faint scent of green apples, I close my eyes and look at her face then try to picture the body beneath the dress. But the body keeps pulling in and out of focus. I open my eyes again. I lie on the bunk like that for the rest of the afternoon, staring at the slats, closing my eyes and letting the pictures come, then opening them again. Dusk falls. The window above me darkens. I hear the grate being dropped on top of the diesel drum. Flywire doors are squeaking, the dog is barking. Everything seems a long way away.

two

During the days that follow we are divided into groups.
I go with the writers, she goes with the actors; there are
musicians too, and painters. All over the oval small groups
sit around in circles with Polly flitting about between
them. The actors are gathered way over there near the
changing shed—I can only catch a glimpse of the back
of my partner's head. They have already broken the ice, I
can see them talking animatedly, but Polly has to help us
by setting up a game. Under her instructions we arrange
our chairs in a circle and then one of us is given a ball, a
medium-sized plastic ball with a tropical fruit motif on
it. The person must throw the ball to someone else in the
circle, but only, as we realise after two false starts, after
saying the first sentence of a story. The person who catches
the ball must then provide the next sentence and so on.

It's a story game, says Polly. The first player is an elderly man with a grey beard and his sentence is: As I walked out that day the air was crisp and clear. When it gets to me my sentence is: She took me by the hand and led me down the steps. It seems to go on forever. Polly has left us to our own devices and gone over to the painters, we don't know whether we are supposed to find our own ending or wait till she comes back. After flitting around the painters; she goes over to the musicians. I am now on my third sentence—everyone is getting restless. By the time Polly returns to our group some people have got bored with the game and have started talking among themselves. Please, says Polly. The story ends in the hands of a very young woman with short cropped hair who speaks her sentence with a little quaver in her voice. Polly applauds with short sharp movements, rapping the four rigid fingers of one hand against the four rigid fingers of the other. Some in the group briefly applaud too.

I look across to the actors. They are doing some sort of performance now; she is acting out a scene with another woman and all the actors watching are falling about laughing. Now, says Polly, drawing my attention away: I have here a list of possible subjects that you may choose to work on. Please pass it around. If a topic interests you, write your name in the column provided. One topic only per person, please, but be sure to give a second preference in case your first choice is taken. The sheet of paper is handed around the circle. I choose A Short History of Laburnum, a suburb not far from where I grew up, and hand it on to the next person. Some people spend a long time over their choices; others, not many though, seem to be treating the whole thing as a joke. Polly has already made a mental note of these people and deliberately distracts herself when one of them giggles over the list. If the game had created a sense of camaraderie in the group then already it is dissipating; sideways glances are being exchanged, some older members have become deliberately aloof—they fill in their name and pass on the sheet without looking at their neighbour—while still others just look confused and afraid they may do the wrong thing.

The list finally ends up back with Polly, who quickly runs an eye over it. It's so hot out here in the centre of the oval that I'm afraid one of us is going to faint. I want to ask again—What is this all about?—but I'm afraid that if I do Polly will finally lose patience with me. I've begun to feel sorry for her—it's not her fault, she's been left to organise the whole thing herself—and I don't want to make things worse. I look around the circle, wondering if anyone might be brave enough to ask the question instead. My eye falls on a red-headed young woman in a big straw hat. Jane Austen, I think. She has her legs just slightly open and I can almost see her knickers. An idea suddenly comes to me and I have to hide my smile. I move my eye around the circle: Anton Chekhov, Nikolai Gogol, Robert Louis Stevenson, Heinrich von Kleist. This is very funny. I'm giving them all names. The names come easily to me, I am barely thinking—Christina Stead, Henry Lawson, Elizabeth Jolley, Patrick White—and the excitement I'm getting out of doing this is almost too hard to contain. I go around the whole circle—Polly is talking, explaining what we are supposed to do next—and effortlessly I give a name to each member of the group. I finish with Jorge Luis Borges to my left, a middle-aged man with over-shampooed hair and sharp birdlike features, who, perhaps sensing something strange, glances briefly at me before turning to Polly again.

And so, says Polly, I think you'd agree that this presents a fabulous opportunity for you all. She has just explained the whole thing. Even the cynics, those who laughed at the list, have now become respectfully silent. Any questions? asks Polly. I have a question but I can't ask it. Polly smiles and moves away: we are free to go back to our vans.

I'm always missing something—I have missed something again. I don't listen properly, I am always thinking about something else. Long after the other writers have moved away from the circle I remain there thinking about all this and am still thinking about it when I see Polly glaring at me from over near the boundary. I pick up my chair and stack it in its place and go back to the van.

That evening I ask my partner how was her day and she asks me how was mine. I tell her everything—the ball game, the talk, the list, the afternoon staring at the wall—but the more I tell the more depressed I get. She on the other hand can't contain her excitement—some of the best actors from town are here, people she's always wanted to work with, they've already formed a small company and started devising a show, soon they'll be touring, it's everything she's ever wanted. I listen to her and watch her moving around the caravan as if she has suddenly become someone else. I explain to her that from my point of view the work I will be doing will not be so exciting, but she just laughs me off. You're right, I say, I know, I say, I'm just feeling a bit lost, that's all.

That night we sleep back to back. I hear her gentle breathing. I look up through the crack in the curtain at the deep black star-filled sky. Strange muffled sounds from the other caravans drift towards me. I close my eyes. We are walking along the edge of a cliff-top, below us in the void a flock of birds are wheeling around. I lean over to kiss her but she jumps aboard one of the birds and flies away. The other birds follow; little pebbles tumble down the cliff-face and echo far below.

Next morning when I wake up she is already gone. They are devising their *bouffon* piece in the church hall of a town somewhere nearby. She has left a note on the sink, she wants me to ask about the washing: Is there somewhere we can wash our clothes? I go back to bed and masturbate then take her socks and undies and mine to the toilet block where I wash them in the basin. I hang them on the chrome rail at the front of the caravan. Breakfast is being served over near the players' gate. You have to take your bowl and plate, spoon and knife, and from the trestle table covered with a white plastic table-cloth you can choose from Cornflakes or Weeties and cold white bread toast with strawberry jam or Vegemite. I take my bowl of Weeties back to the van.

On the bed is a small package: a Tudor 5mm ruled ninety-six-page exercise book, a Pilot Fineliner pen and a small kit in a plastic pocket with a sticker on the outside that says 'Laburnum'. I open the plastic pocket and look at the kit. It is two A4 pages, stapled together; it tells me something about Laburnum and has a bad copy of a photograph of the local primary school stapled to the top of the second page. It gives me guidelines to follow ('feel free to use your subject in a creative way') and has a short reading list at the end which has, however, been hastily crossed through.

It's not easy getting started. At about eleven o'clock that morning I write *Laburnum*, then, *Laburnum is a small suburb in Melbourne's east*, then *Laburnum is a small suburb in Melbourne's east, perhaps best known for the railway station bearing its name*—then quickly scratch my pen through that and start again. This goes on until lunchtime when quarter-cut ham sandwiches are informally served out on the oval. I linger too long over my sandwich and by the time I sit down in the caravan again more than half the day is gone.

On a night of driving rain, in the depths of a bitter winter, in the year 1851, a bullock dray stopped in a clearing in the outer east of Melbourne and a tall figure in a wide-brimmed hat was seen dismounting and hobbling his beasts before offering his hand to the figure still seated above him, wrapped head to toe in a grey blanket and looking for all the world like a monk. Over the course of the next hour or so the two figures worked slowly and methodically in the relentless rain, pitching a tent of basic design, its guy ropes lashed to the trees around. Under this shelter the tall figure then lit a smoky fire and a blackened tin was placed upon it.

During the following days, as the rain eased and the clouds scudded high above, Ernest Fairweather and his wife May began to make of that clearing a small settlement, a settlement that eventually was to open up the entire eastern corridor and lay down the foundations of the modern-day suburb of Laburnum.

Ernest Fairweather was a philologist who had been educated at Eton and Cambridge until the incident with the gardener

Ernest Fairweather was a draper's son and a draper himself who, until the downturn in the drapery market, seemed destined for a long and prosperous career. He met May shortly after his arrival through a mutual friend of his uncle's. Quickly realising that it was either a struggling drapery business in the harsh world of the goldfields or a life lived more peacefully and at one with nature in a place more remote, he took the track east from Melbourne one day, declaring that wherever they were when the sun went down would be the place to settle.

It was in the garden of May's grandmother's house in Cheltenham that she first saw laburnum, with its dark trunk and pendulous yellow flowers, and it always reminded her of those happy times when, waking in the morning and pulling aside the curtains, she would see the bees buzzing around the racemes and the geese waddling up the path to the gate. And though she was a long way now from Cheltenham and the vegetation here was of a wholly different character it gave her great comfort to know that, when her husband had asked her what they might call their little settlement, she had said 'Laburnum' and he had agreed.

Can I come in? A young man is standing on the step, looking in through the flywire door. I'm Shannon, he whispers, I was opposite you, at the table. I push my papers aside. He's a thick-set young man with greasy shoulder-length hair, a black t-shirt and beige cargo shorts that show off his puffy white calves. He is carrying the silver bladder from a wine cask and has blown it up like a football. To make it easier to pour, he says. He steps inside. I got it when they were cleaning up, he whispers, and he gives me a stupid grin. I gesture for him to sit then get two cups from the cupboard, one with circumnavigating brown stripes, the other with Garfield the cat on it. You asked that question, didn't you, he says, about the cleaning things? He holds the bladder over my cup: I don't know how you did that. I sit down opposite him. I said 'young man' but now I'm not so sure. He's the one I called Georg Büchner. He has a fat, pasty, sickly-looking face and big brown bug-like eyes. So what's your question? I ask.

He's talking then, very suddenly, very quickly, too quickly for my hazy head, still roaming as it is in the bush around my imagined Laburnum. He feels very strongly about what he's saying, he says, he doesn't want to get me into any trouble and obviously he realises that under the circumstances we have to be careful about how we voice our opinions, but, he reminds me, we have rights as much as the next person, we're not just putty to be moulded this way or that, we can't just accept the situation without any protest at all, as it seems the others are already doing. I give him a questioning look. In the first place, he says, the whole process was supposed to be based on choice, wasn't it? You were actually asked to choose your topic, admittedly from the choices made available to you, but the element of choice was still inherent in the system. You have a problem with your choice of topic? I ask. I have chosen a topic, he says, but now I've found out there were at least three other topics that were, well, I won't say similar— that were almost identical. Obviously this is designed to set up some kind of competitive environment, where one piece is somehow going to be judged up against another.

I think this is very unfair. If not misguided. Surely if they are trying to find a way to deal with us it won't be found by perpetuating this overly competitive environment, where we are forced to operate almost in competition with one another for—as they never tire of telling us—the very limited resources available. You think they're trying to find a way to deal with us? I ask. There are too many of us, says Büchner: isn't that obvious? I look at him curiously. It's like the kangaroo *(The kangaroo?)*: we clear the land, give them green pasture; they feed voraciously on it and breed like rabbits. There are just too many kangaroos. But we can't kill them, can we? They're too important—to the tourist industry, the national psyche, the way we are seen in the eyes of the world. So we protect them. But in the end there are just too many kangaroos and not enough grass left to go around. A solution has to be found. You see what I'm saying? We've eaten out the paddock, so they've moved us on, to 'greener pastures'—hah! Well, they can't cull *us*, can they?—much as I'm sure they'd like to. You think we're here because we're artists? I ask. Obviously, he says. There's no question, he continues, that we've produced an excess of well-educated but ultimately disaffected individuals who with little or in some cases no talent at all set themselves up as artists and then as artists continually bleed a system which, in turn, perversely, has been set up to be bled by them—and the fact is, I don't deny it, I've stood by that door too, my friend, cap in hand, asking for a handout; we all have, we're all part of the same corrupt system, that's why we're here. We've all filled in their forms at some stage or other, we've all given them our details, told them what we'd like to do with their money. In my case I've done that—what? I don't know—at least half a dozen times—I'm only twenty-six—and as many times they've knocked me back. So yes, they knew my address, they knew where to find me—and so, here I am. I've chosen my topic, I've started work on it—good work too, some of my best work—but all the time I can't help thinking: This isn't right, how can I feel like I'm doing original work when already there's someone else dealing with exactly the same topic as me? It's not that I object to being here, he is saying, far from it, the caravan I've got is better than the place I was in. But I still think it's reasonable to ask questions without fear of retribution and suggest ways that things could be improved. For example, I like my caravan, it's good, but I am used to having a bit of garden around me. In the share house where I lived I had a bungalow in the backyard and over the last couple of years I'd made a little garden around it—some vegetables, some herbs, a few flowers—and I suppose I've got used to that. I'd always potter around in there and I found it helped my work. Of course it's not for me to judge how successful or otherwise this work has been but I do think it's laughable, how you can read these articles in the weekend supplements about the parlous state of the fiction publishing industry and then have the very same editors and publishers who are in charge of this industry nod their heads in agreement but continue to ignore the most interesting work in favour of the most bland and boring. But I'm getting off the point—what I was wondering was if you got those cleaning things you asked for?

There's a pause. I look at him. Yes, I say. So the rules aren't that strict after all, he says, almost to himself, stroking his chin-beard like an Oriental, a little twinkle in his eye. He wants to ask Polly if he can cultivate the area around his caravan to plant a garden—this is why he's here, he's wondering how he should approach this request: should he wait for a while first, he says, to see how the scheme is working, or should he put her on the spot now? I can't answer. I feel sick, nauseous. I watch his mouth moving, the spit on his chin. I hear his torrent of words. *Shut up,* I want to say, *just shut up can't you? Just shut up and get out of my caravan!* You'll have to go, I say. I'm looking out the window. I see the actors' Ford Transit van pull up next to the changing shed, see the driver slide the side door open and the actors start piling out. Polly is walking around the boundary fence to greet them. You'll have to go, I say.

The man is chopping the tree in the clearing and the sound of axe on wood rings out through the surrounding bush. The woman is seated under another tree a little way off, brushing away flies with a switch. A man rides up. He is sitting very high in the saddle and has a tall hat on his head. He stops beside the man who lets the axe fall beside him: a heavy, lifeless thing. From inside his jacket the tall-hatted man takes out a roll of paper and hands it down to the man who leans the axe-handle against his leg, wipes his hands on the front of his shirt and takes the paper from him.

By the time I finish putting down these notes and sliding them back into my plastic pocket, evening has fallen. People are gathering for dinner, milling around the trestle tables in the centre of the oval: selecting their food, sitting down to eat. It looks like cold meats and salad. When I sit down beside her among the noise and clatter she throws an arm theatrically around me and pulls me to her and kisses me on the cheek. She's telling her friends she loves me. She fills my plate with food like a mother and sets it down before me. She asks me how was my day? I say not good, I had trouble getting started—but softly, for her ears alone. I then ask her how was hers. She tells me, I listen, but it's all very fast and full of too much detail. Then she's lowering her voice too and speaking up close: I've been talking to some of the others, she is saying, and they agree, we think we can get you into our group.

I'm not sure what she means by this but the feel of her warm breath in my ear, the smell on it of freshly chewed lettuce, the gentle stroke of a wisp of hair as she turns away again, it all makes me love her badly. This feeling comes up off me in a wave and she turns and smiles as if having felt it and kisses me on the cheek again. Am I really a writer? Or am I just killing time? A young woman across the table, one of the members of her group, is looking at me curiously, but I can't return the gaze. I look down at my salad and think of Laburnum. Why shouldn't it be a great work, something to be read and reread by genera-tions of readers to come? And if this is not the great work, what *is*?

She wants me to stay, she wants to tell me all about her day, but I want to go back to the van. I stand up. I need to work, I say. Everyone in her group is looking at me—she's been talking about me, I know she has, and now they're all looking at me as if trying to judge the actual me up against the things they've heard. I do my best to return their looks, or rather I glance and smile at each in turn: first one, then the next, then the one after that. Sorry, I say, I'm going back to the van, I need to do some work. I walk away—strange situation!—and am happy with the impression I've left.

The air in the van still smells faintly of the wine Büchner and I had drunk. I squeeze the bladder but this time it really is empty and all I get is wine-smelling air. I sit down at the table. There is no light on inside, they will not see me, so I pull the curtains well apart and look back out onto the oval. Everyone's out there. I see the Transit van being parked on the boundary fence, its headlights on, illuminating the oval. Someone runs a lead out from the changing shed, a Portaflood in their hand. They're preparing for some entertainment. It's all very relaxed, I think, you could even learn to like it. Yes, we needed a change, it's not good to wake up every morning to the same living conditions, the same working conditions— day in, day out—we should always allow room for the unexpected in our lives. It's strange, I never thought of it: I'm an artist and these are my people. We've all been gathered up, fished out of our nooks and crannies with a net whose weave would catch only us. Somewhere else there might be another oval with tradesmen on it. You delude yourself for so long into thinking you are part of the real world—the world that works, worries, procreates, watches television—and then one day you are reminded that you are not. We represent no-one but ourselves, we are small, hermetic, navel-gazing, self-congratulatory—in the end probably utterly useless. But then just when we have convinced ourselves that that's precisely what we are, along comes someone like Polly. She puts us in a caravan, says we're worth keeping, and brings us here. Small fish scattered in small schools across a vast ocean, netted up and dropped in a hold and made to rub their bodies across each other's. We finally get to see who we really are. And who are we?

I've been staring at the table—at a red wine stain on the laminex—and now I look up again. One of the writers—Fyodor Dostoevsky—is standing up on a chair holding a piece of paper in his hand; one of the actors—Andrew—has the Portaflood trained on him like a spotlight. I can barely make out the sound of Dostoevsky's voice—it's very faint, very far away—but then he stops, and there's a round of applause. He gets down, and another writer gets up. They're doing little performances. Perhaps of the work they wrote today. Each performance ends with a small round of applause.

What are you doing? Polly is standing in the

doorway, looking up through the flyscreen into the caravan. Though the light is off inside I am sitting at the table, lit by the Transit van's headlights streaming in through the open curtains from outside. I don't think it's unreasonable, Wayne, she says, to expect people to participate. I'm not feeling well, I say. Polly looks at me. I've done well to answer like this. I think it's something I ate, I say. This sets her back even further on her heels. I'm sorry, I say, I'll participate tomorrow, I promise; the best I can do tonight is to watch from my window. I've surprised myself, Polly is disarmed, she nods her head in a series of short sharp movements up and down and, having no riposte, she is gone again. When I resume looking out the window I see her walking with quick steps back to the group where now another writer—Helen Garner—is up on a chair, speaking.

It's funny, but by telling Polly I'm not well, I feel it. With the curtains still open and with the headlights still streaming in from the outside I lie down on the bench seat and look up at the ceiling. Outside I can hear the sound of the writers reading, punctuated by applause. Is it too late to change, I think, can I be someone else, can I tell Polly I don't want to do this any more? I feel tired, exhausted; a bit of work, a few glasses of wine, and I can barely keep my eyes open. The beginnings of sentences—new first sentences—for my Laburnum story come to me unbidden, unroll themselves out in my head for a way, then stop. One after another they come, and one after another they go. When she whispers and wakes me I have been asleep for an hour. In my dreams I felt her coming, the rise and fall of the van as she mounted the step in my dream was the rise and fall of a boat in the arm of a lake high up in the mountains where for some reason I was looking for gold. Don't sleep there, she says, come to bed. I sit up. Extraordinary vision. The headlights are still on and out on the oval at least half the community is still watching the writers rise and fall. One gets up, then down, then another, up and down. It looks like it's been going on for years. I think I can get you into our group, she says, closing the curtains: I've spoken to Polly. She turns on the light. It's too sudden, too bright. I've told her we need a dramaturg. A what? I say. A dramaturg, she says, to help us with structure. You can come into town with us, watch us work, write things down, make suggestions.

We lower the table. I make up a bed and we both get into it. The noises outside have stopped, the crowd has broken up—after a while the headlights go out. A gluey silence comes down. I watch her falling asleep. I can almost hear the clash and jangle of relived moments moving through her. She's been making theatre, she's been

41

acting, she and her friends; they have in the few hours they've had together lived and played in a way that to me is unimaginable. I move closer and drape an arm over her and feel her chest rise and fall.

three

Polly is on the step, calling out. I can feel the van rocking and swaying. I'm still in bed—now I remember. I look beside me but she has gone. She got up early, told me she was getting ready and would come back for me later. I fell asleep. Now Polly is on the step. I have already made an exception for you, she is saying, the least you could do is make an effort. I sit up. Please now, she says, Wayne, I've agreed to let you go, but you must still follow some basic rules. Now I remember. I'm going into town with the actors. Yes, I say, I'm sorry, I'll be there in a minute.

She gets off the step and moves away. The van rocks again. I look out through the curtains—the breakfast tables are being cleared. I throw on yesterday's clothes and splash my face with water. There's a small overnight bag with a floral pattern on the floor near the door. I don't know whose it is, but something very strong in me says I can't worry about that now.

Outside, the day's activities have already begun. The writers are turning their chairs into a circle for their morning chat; over at the changing shed a group of painters are each pulling on a pair of white overalls while a woman I've not seen before, her hennaed hair done up in plaits, is opening the first in a row of four-litre paint tins; musicians with their instruments are sitting on chairs in a circle inside the players' gate; and now, over near the scoreboard, against a backdrop of dry paddocks and fences, I can see her group of actors doing their morning exercises, all standing in a row, all moving in time.

I'm halfway across the oval towards them when Büchner calls out. He asks where am I going. I gesture in the direction of the actors on the rise. The Transit van pulls up, driven by the actor introduced to me as Andrew. I turn away from Büchner and jump the fence onto the gravel track that encircles the oval; outside, on the paddocks—the 'other world'—a herd of cows with heavy heads are grazing. The farmhouse I'd seen in the distance on the first day and which I can now see again seems somehow to have got smaller, to have shrunk back into the landscape, and now looks like a little toy house way over there on the horizon. Andrew slides the side door back and says good morning; he's sorry he's late, but the Transit van had been used last night to pick up the shopping and he'd only just finished unloading it. Once Andrew has finished talking—he talks very fast, I think: will I have to think this fast too?—she introduces me to everyone. This is our writer, Wayne, she says. I nod and smile. One by one she works her way around the group—there are eight in all. One by one she tells me their names and one by one I forget them. I look at the face, even sometimes for a moment look into its eyes, I listen to the name, I nod my head and smile, but when it's over and I scan back through the faces I can't remember what they are called. Wayne's going to help us with story and structure, she says, and I smile and nod my assent.

Andrew holds the door open and we all get inside. She sits in the front. It's crowded in the back, we all sit squashed up on the bench seats and spend some time sorting out each other's seatbelts. We are just about to go when the door slides back and Polly pokes her head in. Ah, good, she says, you've got him. The woman next to me grabs me tight, holds me too hard, hugs me, I suppose is the word, and says, laughing: Yes, I've got him! Everyone, including Polly, either smiles or laughs. She looks up at Andrew. Did you get the lunches? she asks. Andrew nods. All right then, she says, off you go. She's about to shut the door on us but then I lean forward. Polly, I'm sorry, I say, I'm a bit confused: does this mean I'm finished with Laburnum? She looks at me. Everyone has gone very quiet.

It's a genuine question, I really am confused. She looks at me, I look back at her, but the trouble is she is wearing a low-cut top, red, she is leaning over, and even though I don't look at her cleavage the effort I make in trying not to means my eyes go all shifty and then, what's worse, suddenly lock piercingly on to her eyes: I know if I break the stare between us I will look down, I will look down at her cleavage and everything, everything will be lost. I'm not sure whether I am still supposed to continue with my Laburnum piece, I say. I can see a flush rising in her cheeks. Her eyes seem to be almost quivering. We'll discuss that later, she says. She doesn't break the stare. I pull my top lip down and nod my head rapidly up and down. I then turn and look out the window as if a bird has just flown past. Polly slides the door back and it closes with a thump.

We start driving. We circle the gravel track of the oval two thirds of the way around and come out onto a rough dirt road. The writers are huddled together in their circle, the painters are preparing the west wall of the changing shed, the musicians have split into little duets and quartets and set themselves up here and there around the boundary. It's a peculiar sensation, looking back at all this, all the more peculiar because as I look back at it I think: That's where I live now, that's my home. Between some caravans makeshift washing lines have been hung, some now have old tarpaulins stretched out in front of them like open-air annexes; from this distance you can see very clearly the pattern of paths and gathering places where the grass has already been trampled to dirt.

We're now on the road back to the highway. Andrew has turned the radio on, it blares out a loud pop tune, everyone in the back screams in protest and he changes it to the classical station. We bump along the road; the air-conditioning is on, it's very cool in the back; the car is new and there's a strong smell of lemon air freshener. I look out the window but there is little to see: dry paddocks, fences, a few trees, some cows. The woman next to me asks me a question but I don't hear it. She repeats the question— Are you going to be with us for a while?—and then adds her name. I'm Marti, she says. I'm Wayne, I say. I don't know, I add, this is all new to me. She smiles. Marti. I say it over a few times to myself. Is it going well? I ask. Yes, she says. I nod. Then suddenly everything inside the Transit van changes, the bumping and shuddering stops, we're on the main road, the classical music from the radio seems to swell up and lift us all into a new place. I suddenly feel good, about everything. That's better, I say to Marti, and she smiles at me.

Perhaps it has all turned out for the best? Perhaps this is where I was destined to go? I feel good among these people; I am not one of them, certainly—I am of their genus but not of their species—but I am able to take something from them, something I've not felt before, the sense of not being alone. There is also a sense of freedom, release. I am moving, I am no longer still. And then it strikes me as I think these thoughts—looking out the window, past Marti's head, at the fences swooping past—that yes, in fact, we *are* free, we must be, we, the nine of us, eight actors and a writer, are driving in a Transit van down a country road; Andrew has the keys, has his hands on the wheel, he can do what he likes, he can drive and keep driving, far from here, can pull up, let's say, somewhere way up the coast, in a carpark at the top of the cliffs, and we can all get out and walk down the track and there at the bottom a white beach will stretch out before us, book-ended by rocky promontories, and not a soul in sight.

We're slowing down. I see a house, then another, then a garage with two petrol pumps, then we turn; I lean unintentionally against Marti then straighten up again. It's a side road on the edge of town, all the houses have low fences and big empty front yards. We turn again, then again. The car stops. Everybody out! says Andrew.

It's an old weatherboard church hall—beside it the stone church has been boarded up. The hall has a newly mowed front lawn with neatly clipped hedges and petunia seedlings along the path. Andrew unlocks the padlock on the front door and then the door itself. We follow him in, carrying milk crates full of props and costumes and a cardboard box with tea, coffee, sugar and milk.

It is dark and musty inside the hall, it smells of old wood and dust and mould. Everyone spreads out; they each seem to know what they are doing. The blinds are drawn up and bright daylight floods in, a circle of chairs in front of the raised stage at one end are pushed back against the wall; I follow her out into the little kitchen at the back. There are benches, cupboards, a kettle, an old fridge, a stove. The stove doesn't work but sitting on top of it is a microwave oven. The door to the backyard has been opened to let in the air—a couple of the actors have already taken a chair each out there and started smoking. I fill the kettle—the water at first runs brown—and put it on. When I go back into the hall about half a dozen of the actors are playing a game of soccer with a blue plastic ball. I go back outside to smoke.

At ten o'clock Andrew calls us all in. I hadn't thought of it before but now I realise he's the director. He outlines what we are going to do today, introduces me again and suggests that for today at least I just watch the work and take notes—we will discuss the structural possibilities at more length later. I suddenly realise I have not brought a pen and paper—or rather, realise that I *should* have brought a pen and paper but have not. I'm about to tell Andrew this when things go very serious; we're all standing in a circle, Andrew says something like 'feet under shoulders' and everyone adjusts their position slightly. I do what I think I am supposed to, like everyone else I stare at an imaginary spot on the floor in the centre of the circle and let my arms fall by my side. We all do this for some time. Then suddenly everyone jumps forward and makes a loud *Huh!* sound. I do that too, but a little late; the circle breaks up, people start shaking their limbs, making sounds with their lips and tongues, walking about.

I don't have a pen and paper. I go up to her and in a jokey, coquettish way tell her I've been a bad boy and not brought my writing equipment. She giggles at me then pulls me aside and takes me out the back into the kitchen. On a shelf in one of the lower cupboards she finds some scrap paper (it's from an old dot matrix printer with the holes down either side—on the used side I can see what looks like a church group's financial records) and then in the cutlery drawer an old blue biro. I test the biro, give it a shake, and eventually get it working. She goes back into the hall. I take my pen and paper outside and sit on one of the smokers' seats.

The backyard is mostly concrete, surrounded by a low corrugated iron fence, with a toilet down the end. Someone has long ago shifted an old cupboard out there and it still stands where it was first dropped; the cheap veneer has lifted, like a shell prised open, and the chipboard underneath has begun to swell and split. An old crystal vase stands on top of it, the bottom third stained inside by what I imagine is years of rainwater evaporating, filling, and evaporating again. Above me the sky is very blue. I can hear the occasional sound of a truck out on the highway and the hiss of airbrakes as they slow down into town. In this mood I am tempted to write something, and I actually set the bundle of scrap paper on my knees and take up my pen, but then she is at the back door, calling me in.

Inside the hall a rough performance area has been marked out with white tape. At first I am a little confused as to where I should stand, where the audience is; I move first down one end of the hall, then the other, then I realise they are playing 'in the round'. A chair and table have been placed on their marks in the centre of the hall and on the table is an old-fashioned telephone with its cord dangling onto the floor. Around the playing area various other small props and costume items have been laid out. The wooden floor of the hall is polished and very shiny and there is something very satisfying, visually, I tell myself, in this arrangement of objects on it. The actors have spread themselves out around the hall, some in groups, some alone, some preparing their bodies or their voices, some going through their cues with their colleagues. One actor, a very tall thin young man, is standing on the raised stage area on his own, rolling his spine down until his fingers touch the floor then rolling it back up again. Andrew comes up to me and offers me a chair—to get me out of the way, I presume—then calls the group into the central playing area where he quickly goes over what they are to do and what they are hoping to achieve with this run. Andrew finishes. Everyone goes back to their places. I put my paper on my lap and take the top off my pen.

The performance begins. It's confusing from first to last, but I'm never sure, at any point in it, whether this confusion is my fault or theirs. An actor sits at the table. The phone 'rings', the actor picks up the receiver, listens, then talks into it. But the trouble is he's talking gibberish, he's not trying to make sense in the normal sense of the word but is by his intonation and inflection trying to make a more phenomenological sense. His gestures are big (he waves his free hand often) and his face-pulling almost cartoon-like. He hangs up the phone and suddenly jumps up and addresses me, the audience, in a very animated fashion, but alas still in gibberish so that I don't understand a word he is saying. He comes right up close, waves his arms about, backs off then comes up close again. It seems like the phone call has upset him and that that's what he's going on about but all I am really conscious of are the little drops of spit that keep flying out of his mouth. Then he's gone. He's taken the chair, two other actors quickly and efficiently remove the table and the scene, apparently, changes. A man and a woman are walking, perhaps in a park.

I can't do it any more. I'm looking but I am not seeing. The couple are walking in the park but I can't go with them. Some of the other actors, while waiting for their cues, are glancing across at me, wondering what I am thinking. I go to write something down, anything, but the pen doesn't work; I shake it and scribble hard up on the top right-hand corner of my paper and the ink starts flowing again. Some actors are still glancing at me. The scene has changed again. She this time is on all fours playing an animal, perhaps a dog, yes, a dog, because all of a sudden she's barking at me. I laugh, then make the note: *dog, good*. It's terrible. I don't know what to do. For a little while I just scribble some gibberish of my own on the paper while feigning interest by leaning forward and smiling with a fixed, gormless smile. But it's all stupid, it makes no sense, I don't know why I'm here. I keep trying to understand what I'm seeing because I know when they are finished they will ask me questions about what I've seen but my mind keeps pulling in and out of focus.

They've brought the table and the telephone back and now the actor who answered the telephone earlier is interviewing, apparently, another actor who is sitting across the table from him. I watch them acting, very loudly, very boisterously, very *pretentiously*, and listen to their theatrical gibberish. What has happened? Why am I here? Did I do something wrong? Scene by scene some kind of story unfolds in front of me but I don't know what the story is. I make notes with my pen but they are just stupid things I am saying, written for the sake of writing something. I try to keep focus on the things unfolding in front of me but it's as if my look keeps ricocheting off them and landing somewhere else. I look at the two actors now entering as drunks, and the next thing, I am seeing in my mind's eye Jane Austen's knickers. I can't bury myself down into the moment—perhaps I have never been able to—I can't dig down and get stuck and let its minutiae cling to me. I skip like a stone across the surface of things,

I am not grounded, earthed; I ramble or lurch from one moment to the next like a drunk. It strikes me that what is happening here, that what is happening back at the oval, that what is happening, now, in my head, is all designed to tell me, again, how utterly adolescent we are, that no matter how painfully we try to make an impression, how desperately we try to prove that we are worthwhile, that we have something to say, that we belong *(Belong!)*, that we are grown-ups now, that we have found meaning, culture, put down our roots, that we are making art, that it all makes sense, we are in fact nothing but distracted children, reaching for one toy while discarding the other, looking up for approval from above, smiling when we get it, bawling when we don't. What is this moment here—this *bouffon* performance, this non-writer taking notes—what if not a contrived collaboration of the stupid with the dumb?

Then suddenly the actor is standing in front of me again, the same as at the beginning, addressing me directly. I know my eyes have glazed over and I try to bring them back into focus. He's winding things up. The performance is over, there's a moral conclusion, they all come on and bow, I put down my pen and clap my hands. Now we'll break for lunch, says Andrew, do you want something from the shop? I must be looking at him stupidly because after a moment he explains himself: Just because we've brought sandwiches doesn't mean we have to eat them. This is no explanation. There's a takeaway up the road, he says. Two dim sims, I say. Steamed or fried? says Andrew. Fried, I say. Fried, he says. They all leave.

I go out the back and sit in the sun. It's hot out there now, not like the morning; I shift the chair into the shade. I can hear the actors leaving, their voices trailing off down the street; they're all excited, they haven't come down. I light a cigarette and look at my notes—it's a fiasco. I can barely read my writing and what I can read I don't understand. One line says: *Take part rubbish man good.* I don't know what that means.

There's a sound inside the hall, then footsteps approaching across the timber floor. A man appears in the kitchen doorway. Who left the door open? he says. I think he means the back door, the door he's standing in, and I'm about to say I did—then he says: Anyone can just walk in off the street and take what they like—and I realise he's talking about the front door, the one with the padlock, the one facing the street. The others have just gone down to the shops, I say, they won't be long. Well, they should have locked it, he says. But I'm here, I say. Doesn't matter, he says. He's a craggy-faced man in his fifties, dressed casually but neatly, like a farmer who has just come into town to go to the bank. It's a stupid arrangement anyway, he says. I don't know what he's talking about. He has a bunch of keys hanging off a clip on his belt. Are you the caretaker? I ask. Yes, I'm the caretaker, he says, and if it was up to me you'd all be packed off back to the city where you belong. He needs to get something off his chest; I put my paper and pen down on the ground beside me. The caretaker meanwhile makes himself look busy: he brings a broom out from the kitchen and sweeps the concrete path, he jags some spiderwebs out from under the eaves, he opens the doors of the rotting cupboard one by one and checks to see if anything has been left inside, he takes down the old crystal vase, turns it this way and that, then puts it back again. I mean, he says, while doing these things, I've got nothing against you people personally, it's no concern of mine what you do with your time—my sister Shirley paints, she's had pictures in the hairdresser's—but you can't just trample over people like that. In what way have we trampled over you? I ask. The caretaker is taken aback by this, he wasn't expecting me to speak, I was going to be his audience: he looks at me briefly then goes back to his pseudo-chores.

It takes a little while to gather momentum but soon he is telling me a story. He's a farmer, has been all his life, his father and his father before that ran cattle on a property just out of town. I think it's easy being a farmer: I read the papers, watch the television, see farmers on their motorbikes and tractors, but really I have no idea what it's like, I just can't possibly imagine the hours, the sweat, the labour these farmers put in and then how little help they get. To expect any meaningful government subsidy is like asking for blood from a stone, he says. If there's a drought, he is saying, or a flood, he says, then guaranteed you'll see a government bigwig with a flash-looking hat sweep through here saying how much relief they'll give us but then just as quickly they're gone again and no talk ever about what good it's going to do us, how the money's going to be spent, whether it's anywhere near enough to compensate us for the damage done by a spiteful, hateful bitch called Nature. I'm not saying we're anything special, he says—he'd be the first to admit that he's done things wrong, made mistakes, that it's not always been the fault of the government or God. But, he says, closing the door of the shed, look around here now, look what's going on, and tell me who's getting the rough end of the stick? When the farm started to go bad, he is saying, neither he nor his wife were expecting any handouts. Jude was a church-going woman, like her mother before her, so when the minister said he needed someone to do some handyman chores around the place and would pay just under twenty dollars an hour for it, I wasn't afraid to put up my hand. Mind you, this is on top of getting up at five, sometimes four-thirty, for milking and on top of the weekend work I was already doing trying to drag another dollar out of that thankless soil. So when the farm collapsed—by collapse I mean when we went to see Dom at the bank like we'd done a hundred times before and for some reason that I couldn't figure out at the time he acted like we had the plague—when the farm collapsed and we were forced to sell (we got nothing for it but the debts we owed and a nest egg the size of a sparrow's) I kept the handyman job at the church and tried to make as much work as I could from it (I don't mind saying) by always finding something else that needed fixing or changing or whatever. So that was all right. But then the scandal broke.

It isn't possible to stop him now, or even divert him from his course. He has taken a chair out of the shed— an old '70s style armchair with brown foam cushions and curved wooden arms—and set it in front of me. Sometimes he sits on the front edge of this chair, sometimes he sinks back into it. The minister, he is saying, who, he adds, my wife thought the world of, was, he continues, involved in some scandal that to be honest I'm still not clear on. But anyway, this minister whose name was Stevens was transferred to another parish and another minister whose name was Simmons was appointed to replace him. But this Simmons had been in the job only about a year when a scandal broke over his head too. This time the details were all over the city papers—it involved the young football team he was coaching. Well, after Simmons left, which he inevitably did, the church took stock and thought it might be best to try and stay out of this town for a while. The church was closed, but the church people in the city kept me on so I could look after it, mow the lawns and clean the gutters and so on. That went on for about a year, I was pulling good money, coming down here most days and spending a few hours about the place, with the other advantage being, of course, that although she had no-one to administer the sacrament my wife could still worship every day if she liked—she had the whole place to herself. But neither of us thought this would go on forever, and, sure enough, one day a letter arrived from the church organisation in the city saying the arrangement had to stop. The church was put on the market and sold to a city couple who I still haven't met—apparently they're going to do it up. But luckily for me the church people kept the church hall and kept me on to look after it. At the time the church was sold there were a few local groups using it so it was earning a bit of money for them but of course it was never enough. Don't worry that some of these groups had been using this hall since the day it was built. It's all about money, that's all everything's about now: money, money, money. So when your woman Polly came along and made some inquiries and offered to pay rent on it five days a week for twice the amount the other groups were paying, well, yes, my job was assured, but at the same time there was another slice of town life taken away from us. The Tai Chi ladies still come in on a Tuesday evening but everyone else has gone elsewhere or disbanded.

It's actually hot out here now, stinking hot, the caretaker is sitting in the shade from the shed but I have the sun full on me. He's talking so much and so personally that I feel I can't move without upsetting him in some way. I can feel my face getting sunburnt, can feel the sweat on my brow, my upper lip, the folds of my neck, my arms, my crotch, my legs. I'm holding my hand above my eyes and squinting but I still can't see him properly. He's really venting his spleen now, I can't listen to it all, he's accusing us of all sorts of things, of 'taking over' the town, of 'trampling' on their traditional way of life; I want to respond somehow—I feel helpless, useless—I want to tell him it's not our fault, that we're victims too, we're all victims, we're all trash, we're all getting thrown out of somewhere to be unwelcomed somewhere else, that if I could return everything to how it used to be I would—Don't you think

I've asked questions about all this, I want to say: don't you think *I* think this is all wrong? Is it only you who's been inconvenienced, isn't it hard on everyone?—but I can't get a word in edgeways and then I hear footsteps in the hall.

They're back. Lunch is nearly over. I've done nothing but listen to the caretaker. He's heard the footsteps too and is on his feet now, putting the chair away. I watch him fumbling with the door of the shed and I suddenly feel a great sympathy go out to him. We're rubbish, it's true, over-educated trash, picked up and dumped here onto his old way of life. I see him trying to drag the shed door back across the concrete, hear the scrape, see where the seam of his pants is parting and I want to kill us all, every last one of us, I want to remove us all and all our petty concerns and every last trace of our over-inflated egos not only from his life but the planet.

Two dim sims with sauce, she says, and she hands me a small brown paper bag. The caretaker brushes past—he's going; I listen with one ear turned towards the inside of the hall but he says nothing to Andrew or anyone else and now she is talking to me. Did you do *anything*? she asks, in a low voice. Did I do what? I say. Anything, she says. I smile. Please, I say, and I put one of the dim sims in my mouth. It's the first thing I've eaten since yesterday's dinner—I bite off half in one go. It's an intense, intensely pleasurable sensation: the slight crunch of the crust then the thick glutinous pepper-flavoured filling. I finish the first, lick some of the soy sauce from my fingers, and bite into the second. We start back again in ten minutes, she says, and she goes back into the hall.

I stand in the backyard and eat the second dim sim. I hold the bag close to my nose so as to let the salty aroma of the soy sauce drift up into my nostrils. I hear a plane flying high above—high, high above—and suddenly I don't care about anything. I've been too polite, too accommodating, have not told people what I really think. It's as if we're all involved in some great conspiracy of self-delusion. I bite the dim sim again. Whole perfectly formed sentences flash through my head—perfect, perfect sentences—and all I can think of is the caravan, the paper, the pen, the blinds drawn, the muffled sounds outside, the blowfly buzzing at the window. In the time it has taken to think these thoughts whole paragraphs, now pages, have trooped their way into my head. I lick my fingers. I take the last piece of dim sim and put it in my mouth.

In the hall the last of the chairs are being brought into the circle. People are finishing their chocolate bars and screwing up the wrappers or drinking the last of their cans of drink. Andrew is congratulating everyone on the morning's work, they've sharpened the focus since yesterday, some of the segues are working better, there's a stronger commitment to each moment. Someone suggests they might now reduce the number of props and Andrew takes this on board. She says (she's sitting directly opposite me and her effort to impress me—or *not* impress me— produces a strange new body language in her) that she feels there are still big structural problems in the second half. Andrew agrees, and turns to me. How did you see it, Wayne? he asks.

Long were the days that Ernest Fairweather and his wife worked in that rough clearing, carving out the first beginnings of what was to become the suburb of Laburnum. In steps, by degrees, the hard brown scrub folded back before them, unrolling itself into green. A fine pillar of white smoke rose from the chimney of their rough slab hut and in the cool late afternoons May could be seen sitting outside on the wooden stool, working the udder of their cow, while Ernest lifted up a bundle of chopped wood, stopped, sniffed the air, creased his eyes, listened, then turned and went inside.

Wayne? Andrew is talking again. I look down at my notes. I've taken a few notes, I say, looking at them: but really, overall, I think it's going very well. I look up. Everyone is looking at me. I shift in my chair. Then it comes to me. Very clearly. In great detail. In fact, I hear myself saying, if you want me to be perfectly honest I think you've made a mistake in inviting me here today. It is actually a demonstration of bad faith, of a lack of confidence in the work you are doing. You don't need a writer; in fact, to have a writer somehow take control of what you are doing, to give it shape or structure, as you say, would undermine what should be the basis of the work. Spontaneity, improvisation, play. These are the things that distinguish all great theatre and particularly the *bouffon*. It would be utterly criminal of me to apply some writerly structure to something that should remain fluid and unpredictable, something whose source, whose *truth*, should flow solely from the actors and their instincts, responding sincerely to each moment, unrestrained and free.

I have heard myself say all this, as if listening to someone at the far end of a lecture hall, and now I am listening to the silence that follows. The only face that is not registering deep seriousness is hers: it's hard to read her expression, somewhere between pitying and derogatory, but I know that she knows that all I want is to sit in our caravan and watch the afternoon breeze blow the cheap lace curtain back in rolling little waves. Well, says Andrew, that's honest. That's how I intended it, I say. Does anyone have any questions? he says. They don't. Someone moves their chair and the scraping sound echoes through the hall.

I spend the rest of the afternoon watching them work. I'm just an audience member now, I can do them no harm, but all afternoon I sense a tension between us. I've become the most powerful kind of critic—the one who doesn't care. All their words and actions are performed under the intense indifference of my gaze. The less I study what they're doing—the more I look up distractedly at the ceiling, at the window, at the old pictures of Christ on the wall—the more likely they are to drop a line, fumble a prop, miss a cue. This goes on all afternoon. Eventually, at five o'clock, the things are packed away, the doors are locked and we all pile back into the Transit van. Everyone is seated just as before. It's not hard to read the silence. Then someone says something (I don't catch what it is) and it's as if, like the actors they are, they had all been waiting for a cue. Everyone starts laughing and talking too loudly; witticisms are exchanged, funny voices put on. There is no place for me in all of this and they know it. They are paying me back, I think, they are saying: We don't need you and your comments. They are free again, just like before. I fix a smiling, indulgent look on my face and stare out the window.

When we arrive back at the oval, dinner is being

prepared. The old routine, I think. We've come back, like little homing pigeons or dogs; we could have run but we haven't. I'd forgotten we were free, completely forgotten, just like that, and now here we are, back again. There is no point in me pretending to know what to do with the props or costumes or what else I might do to feel part of the company, I'm no longer part of the company, I've left the company—they know that and so do I. I move away, jump the boundary fence and start to make my way back to my caravan. The sun is low and the light has started to turn. Long shadows streak themselves across the oval, between them vivid patches of yellow sun. A small circle of drummers are playing together under a tree on the rise just around from the scoreboard; the sound drifts out across the camp and lends to it an exotic, faraway feel. By the changing shed wall I can see the painters and their henna-haired supervisor packing away the day's work. Some children are playing cricket on the bare patch of ground between the dinner tables and my caravan; I throw their ball back and walk on. It's the end of the day. What did I do? I joined the actors and went into town. I can still see them now, walking around the oval towards the changing shed where they will store their things for the night. They stop to admire the painters' mural and to talk to them about it. There's a whole scene going on over there now, perhaps a very important scene, perhaps they are planning the design for some lavish theatre production? I've let all that go—was that a mistake? I am walking across the dusty oval to my caravan. The sky is impossibly huge. I want to go along with things, I don't want to make trouble, I want to fit snugly in the hole that's been dug for me. Were I to stand in the street outside our half-demolished house again and were Polly to open the door to our caravan and gesture for us to step inside, I want again to step willingly inside. I want to say: Yes, I'm coming. I want to feel the sway and the rhythm of the road. I want to go where I'm taken.

When I reach the door of my caravan the first thing I notice is that the main door is open and against the fly-wire door a blowfly is insanely buzzing. I open the door and shoo it out. There's a different smell inside. Is someone there? I ask. Yes, says a voice. It's Elizabeth Jolley, the old woman who twice threw the ball to me in the story game. She's sitting up on the top bunk in her pale blue pyjamas with a notepad propped up on her knees. She looks down at me over her reading glasses and gives me a—what is it?—a motherly smile. I'm sorry, she says, it wasn't my decision. An empty plastic pocket, not mine, is on the table. The floral-patterned overnight bag is lying on the floor beside the bunk. I'm happy to sleep up the top, she says.

I'm about to speak, but now Polly is on the step behind me. There's something different about her. This is Gwen, she says. Gwen is going to be staying with you for a while. Polly steps up into the caravan; I step back towards the sink. She can read my face, she knows what I am thinking. The old woman has gathered a blanket up to her neck. At this stage the arrangement is only temporary, says Polly, we have taken delivery today of some new people and until the tents I've ordered arrive I'm afraid we are all going to have to make a few sacrifices. My understanding is that you and your partner—I'm sorry, I've forgotten her name—will both be in town most days now working on your performance and won't be using your caravan anyway so I'm sure you can put up with a guest for a little while, or until the tents arrive at least. Gwen won't take up much room, as you can see. (In fact, yes, I did see, because the old woman, perched up there in the corner of the top bunk, looked like nothing less than a sparrow on a branch, ruffling its feathers, preparing to sleep.) I've spoken to your partner just now and she has no problem with it; it's not my business to pry into your domestic arrangements but I understand that it shouldn't disrupt things too much in the short to medium term. (Does she mean what I think she means, is she flattening her stomach and putting an outstretched hand on it, just

69

below her breasts, for a reason?—and now all of a sudden she is leaning over towards me, very close, her back turned deliberately towards the old woman, speaking in a half whisper...) Please, she says, you don't know how difficult all this is for me; I know you have strong views but all I'm asking is that you be a little patient, I'm doing the best I can. We're looking very closely at each other. Polly, I say, leaning even closer still: I'm sorry, but the trouble is, you see, you've gone and arranged all this but now I'm not sure if the thing with the actors is going to work out and, well, it looks like I might not be going into town during the days after all and if that's the case then the situation here becomes very difficult for me.

Many thoughts are playing across Polly's face now—and not all of them to do with the topic at hand. It's like there is a row of thoughts in her head waiting to be processed and that the one dealing with me and my inability to work with the actors must now make its way patiently to the front of the queue. But you *have* to go into town, she says. But I can't, I say. I stuck my neck out for you, she says. I know that, I say, but it hasn't worked out. This is ridiculous! she says, you're all acting like children! That's because you treat us like children, I say. She looks over her shoulder at Elizabeth Jolley to see if she's listening—of course she is, but with a look that says: I'm

70

not. All right, whispers Polly, leaning close: if that's the way it is, you're going to just have to work it out between yourselves—but I'm warning you now, the tents might not arrive tomorrow, or for that matter the day after, the tents might not arrive for a month; Gwen needs somewhere to stay, and in the meantime this is where she is staying.

I don't know if my look lets Polly know that I accept what she has said because I know I'm not looking at her the right way. When I'm not looking at her lips—very red, almost bloodied, and moving in an invertebrate animal kind of way—I'm trying self-consciously *not* to look at the rest of her and am instead looking past her through the flywire door to the oval, the neighbouring caravans and the low-down strip of candescent sky. Yes, I say—and as an afterthought—I'm sorry the actors thing didn't work out. We lock eyes: time stands still. I know you went out of your way, I say, I know you've done everything you can, we really are dependent on you now, we're in your care, we're all useless without you, that's why you've taken us in, and now the obligation is on us to do something useful in return. I'm not sure that I've ever seen Polly smile—really smile, I mean. But now she smiles. Good, she says. She steps out of the van. The flywire door squeaks and slams.

I'm sorry, says Elizabeth Jolley. It's no trouble, I say. She puts aside her notebook and clips the pen to the cover.

(She must have brought her own notebook: why didn't I think of that?) I'm sorry to hear your business with the actors didn't work out, she says, that's a great pity. It is, I say, sitting down at the table: but perhaps it was doomed from the start. In what way? she asks.

It's a little while before I realise what is happening, that I am engaging in a conversation with this old woman on our bunk, but by the time I do I feel powerless to stop it. Well, in the first place, I say, because we shouldn't mix work and play. What do you mean? she asks. My partner is an actor, I say, and even though we ourselves feel perfectly comfortable about working together I think the others in the group tend to project a level of meaning onto the relationship that perhaps isn't there. That's unfortunate, she says. But the main thing, I say, is that the role of the writer is so badly defined. In what way? she asks. Well, don't you think that when we put things down into words we lock them down in some way, I say, give them permanence? Isn't that the main reason we do what we do? But the act of performance, I continue, this has nothing to do with being in a fixed spot, doing or saying a fixed thing; a performance is the brush of a butterfly's wing against the sand, it is *impermanent*, that's what defines it. The idea of giving what should ideally be an improvised performance some kind of structure, or worse, a script, is a bit like telling an abstract expressionist painter to become an architect. I'm sorry, she says, I didn't follow all that. She is leaning over looking down the aisle between the bunks at me. I look up at her, looking down at me—I can't save it now, it's become a conversation, there's no point trying to resist. I get up from the table and lean against the sink.

Are you a writer? I ask. (*Another* writer, I want to say.) The old woman sinks back into her pillows. I write children's books, she says, for children. She fiddles with the blanket. I used to work with an illustrator, she says—Mary Gruben, you might know the name—but unfortunately Mary passed away a couple of years ago and I have since been working on my own. Polly thinks she can team me up with one of the painters here, it's a nice idea, a young man who has apparently done some magazine illustrations, and we did get together a few days ago and he did show me some of his work but—I shouldn't be telling you all this—I was very unhappy about it. My relationship with Mary, you see, this had been built up over years—we first started working together in our early thirties—and you don't just replace a working relationship like that overnight. I don't blame Polly herself for this, she's doing what she can, she's just a functionary really, but it does show a certain amount of naivety, I think, to expect a collaboration just to happen, simply because a couple of people are put together willy-nilly. There's a pause. Tell me, I ask, if you don't mind: did you happen to apply for any government money recently? For the last three years, she says, since Mary died, I have applied each year for what I would call a very modest amount to develop work that might succeed independent of any illustrations but unfortunately each application has been unsuccessful, yes. And now you're here, I say. And now I'm here, she says.

It's almost dark outside. I look out through the curtains above the sink. Just about everyone is out there now, sitting down to dinner at the trestle tables that are all lined up in rows out in the centre of the oval. It's time to eat, I say, can I help you down? I'd rather just stay here, she says. Can I get you something then? I ask. That would be nice, she says. You're welcome to stay, I say, stopping in the doorway: I'm sure we can work something out. She smiles. I go outside.

It's already very lively out there in the centre of the oval and as I walk from my caravan towards it I can see that every day, every night, little by little, in spite of everything, the awkwardnesses between us are diminishing. The groups are no longer so clearly defined—writers sit with painters, painters with musicians—and within each group, and between them, a lively conversation is taking place. The table is spread with candles, the wine casks are handed around; as I approach the tables Büchner the talker comes towards me with a cask of red wine in one hand and a plastic cup in the other. I don't hear what he says at first—I've already held my cup out and had it filled and taken my first sip before I do—because all I am really conscious of is the group of actors all gathered down there at the end of the far table, talking among themselves and occasionally glancing over in what I imagine is my direction. Well, Büchner is saying, have you seen it yet? I don't know what he's talking about: I don't think I want to know. It's just like I was saying, he's saying, you don't have to lie over and let them tickle your belly—if you feel strongly about something you've just got to speak up for it. He's talking about his garden. I told her very clearly, he says, you've got to make some allowances for individual creativity. You can't just give us a plastic pocket with a piece of paper in it and expect us to work. The garden's not an indulgence, it's a part of the creative process. You got your garden, I say. After a bit of sweet-talking, he says, smiling: I spent the afternoon setting it up—but it's still early days, of course. You've got to come and have a look. I will, I say. Büchner suddenly grabs my elbow and turns me aside and whispers in my ear. She's vulnerable, he says, she's running the show on her own, if you put enough pressure on her you can get what you want. Personally, he continues, I think we've got to stop thinking of ourselves as victims, outcasts—we've got to turn it back around. We're important members of the community, we are an essential part of the *cultural and economic* fabric of the country, they know that, they *have* to take us seriously. He lets go of my elbow again. You must come and see my garden, he says, it's just a start, but I think you'll like it.

I tell him I will come and see his garden tomorrow and I half raise my plastic cup towards him as if to toast the fact. He walks back to his chair. I watch his fat arse kicking out from side to side and the backs of his sandals flapping. I move to the nearest table, take a plate and fill it with food. I can feel some of the actors still looking at me. Polly is sitting down the end of one table and her look, too, I feel. There are sausages and vegieburgers; I put one of each on the plate. All these people, with nowhere else to go. I go back to my van.

Gwen is asleep. She's sunk down into the pillows and her head has flopped to one side. The curtains on the window next to her are open and her pale old woman's face shines like a moon in the moonlight. I sit down at the table and eat the meal, glancing up at her occasionally. I'll probably get into trouble for this, I think; I should be out there being social. Then, like the realisation of a prophecy, my partner is at the door. What's wrong with you? she whispers. I gesture towards the bunk and shrug as if to say: Isn't that obvious? But I thought you were going to be working with us, she says. I still have the cup of red wine with me *(To accompany the meal, I think)*: I take a sip then cut the sausage and put a piece in my mouth. She looks at me and smiles. You're a strange one, she says. I don't speak, I don't answer her, but what I do is I look up from my meal and look around me theatrically, first to Elizabeth Jolley, sleeping, then to the crowd gathered out on the oval as if to indicate to her what I personally think when I hear the word 'strange'. Then I go back to my meal. It's a pity you're not coming with us, she says. You'll be better off without me, I say. Will you be all right, though? she asks. She's looking up at the bunk. I nod and smile. I'm starting to think about Laburnum. They're all talking about what you said today, she says, meaning the actors. I don't reply. She comes over and kisses me. I look up from my sausage. It's going to be good, she says, everything, it's going to be good.

She goes. The flywire door creaks, hisses and shuts. The drummers have started up. The air is very warm and still. I can hear Elizabeth Jolley breathing. I push aside my plate and pull the Laburnum folder back across the table in front of me. There are little specks of blowfly shit on the cover. I wipe them off with my thumb. So, I say, out loud, and then again, in my head, to myself: So.

four

I wake up late with a hot shaft of sun on my cheek. She is already gone. The sheet is crumpled around my ankles, I'm bathed in sweat (it's going to be hot, already the caravan feels like an oven); the inside of my mouth feels swollen and I can't lift my head from the pillow. I stare at the woodgrain veneer of the caravan wall, right there in front of my nose. Then I remember the old woman.

You got very drunk, she says. I open my eyes and roll over. Good morning, she says. I pull the sheet back up over me. Good morning, I say. She's already working, propped up on the pillows with her notebook on her knees. Did you sleep all right? she asks. Yes, I say. Your partner's already gone, she says, she said she'll see you this evening. With the sheet still wrapped around me, I rummage through the pile of clothes on the floor, find what I need and get dressed, then splash my face with water in the sink. Have you had breakfast? I ask. No, she says. I look out through the curtains—the last trestle table is just now being carried back to the changing shed. We're too late, I say. She doesn't mind. She looks down at me over her reading glasses and smiles.

I put the bedclothes away and raise the table. My folder has spent the night under the mattress and with the mattress base now become the tabletop again I need only reach out with my free hand and draw it towards me. What is your topic? asks Gwen. A Short History of Laburnum, I say—it's a suburb near where I grew up. And you're making progress? she asks. Yes, I say. I slide the papers out of the folder and start flicking through what I have written. I place the information sheet with the photo attached on the table where I can see it. A long time passes. My stomach grumbles. I can hear the scratch of Elizabeth Jolley's pen.

Later that morning there's a knock at the door. It's Büchner. He gestures for me to come outside. Gwen looks down over her glasses at him, a dark shape behind the flywire. This is Shannon, I say, pointing: Shannon's a writer too. This phrase, 'a writer too', depresses me to no end; it sticks in my throat, starts to burn, then the burning goes down to my stomach. Büchner nods stupidly, then gestures to me again. I look at him, his stupid grin, his greasy hair, his t-shirt hanging out. I need to have a chat with you, he says.

I step outside. The sun is high—it must be nearly midday—and there are no clouds but a few wisps low down in the west. The light is sharp and stings your eyes; I stand in the thin slip of shade along the caravan wall. Büchner, his stupid sloppy t-shirt already dark around the neck and armpits, chooses to stand in the sun. I've got one too, he says. I look at him dumbly. I've got one too, he says. He means an old person. They put him in my caravan yesterday, says Büchner, while I was out; he's been snoring all night—you know him, the guy with the beard. There's a pause. Büchner glares at me. So you're just going to accept the situation? he says, with a ludicrous tone in his voice. I don't know what to say. There's not much we can do, I venture. Büchner looks back at me indignantly. See this? he says—he has half-turned himself around and is now showing me the back of his calf. (It's a bruise, topped by the raw remains of a graze.) Don't worry, I've got photos of it, he says; it's nearly healed now. He turns to face me again. You see, I refused to go; I actually put up a fight. They had to drag me out the door. Do you think we should accept what's going on here without putting up a fight? He's waiting for an answer. What's going on? I ask. This! he says, in a snake-whisper: we're artists—that's why we're here—but how are we supposed to work *like this? (Like what? I think: like what?)* Do you *want* to share your caravan with a writer twice your age? he asks. I'm not sure, I say, it might be good: maybe they intend it as some kind of mentorship? Büchner snorts. Honestly! What kind of work do they expect to get out of us if they're going to saddle us with the older generation? Surely not anything dynamic and original! Do I really need some old stylist looking down over my shoulder, judging what I do, loading me up with all their outdated baggage? How old are you? he asks. Thirty-six, I say. You see, he says, you're not a young writer any more, thirty-five's the cut-off, it's different for you. But I'm prime young writer, says Büchner, I need to protect my branding. I've only got a few years left. The least I can expect is a room of my own.

He has a point, I think, as I stand there looking at him, standing under the blazing sun, sweat now pouring in tiny streams down his forehead and cheeks. But what I don't understand is why he's saying all this to me. Am I supposed to feel sorry for him? Everything about him is pitiful: the hair, the stupid little chin-beard, the t-shirt with the slogan on it, the cargo shorts, the leather sandals. But most of all the idea that we—*we*, of all people—should raise our voices in protest and ask—for what? Quiet time?

Better food? Compensation for our bruises? I'll come over and see your garden later, I say. Büchner is disarmed. He shuffles in the dirt, lifts and drops his shoulders—it was not the garden he'd come to discuss. He's about to speak. I'll come over later, I say.

I step back inside out of the sun and sit at the table— through the curtains I see Büchner walking back across the oval to his caravan. He stops, looks back, then shuffles on. It's all quiet out there now, and deserted. Everything is shimmering under a pitiless sun. The old woman coughs, then asks can I wet the facewasher she is holding out towards me—she has also made a fan from some sheets of notepaper and with the other hand is now fanning herself with it. On a drift of thoughts I put the washer under the tap, squeeze it out and hand it up to her. She lays it on top of her head and resumes fanning herself with the paper. I'm sorry, she says, as I turn back to the table: I know this is awkward—I turn back again—it's not the ideal situation for either of us, is it? With the washer on her head it's hard to take her seriously, but I do. It's not your fault, I say. I don't usually work in the afternoons, she says, I usually sleep, so your time will then be your own. *(Afternoon, I think, yes—it's nearly lunchtime already.)* Would you like to get up and stretch your legs for a while? I ask. Perhaps tomorrow, she says. She falls silent. I look at her with the washer on her head, staring out into space. She's having a thought. After some time staring she picks up her pen and starts writing and then all I can hear is the scratch of the pen and some half-heard sounds from outside.

The washer is a good idea but I don't have another. I splash my face and hair in the sink and go back to the table without drying it. I sit there letting the cool get into my blood. I wipe my hands on my shirt. I look at my papers but there's really no point. The heat coming off the window, even with the curtains closed, is unbearable; the laminex table is warm to the touch. I close my eyes but when I do I don't see Laburnum but Büchner, his sweaty face, his dark underarms, his smug smirk, I even see in my mind's eye his grub of a penis, hiding under a ledge of fat. Everything about him is slippery, odorous, repugnant. I don't care that I have an old woman with a washer on her head sitting on the top bunk of my caravan—this is nothing compared to the nausea I feel looking at Büchner in my mind's eye and hearing him call himself a writer. I try again to think of Laburnum—*When Ernest Fairweather, the draper's son, and his wife, May, first stopped their cart in that rough clearing ten miles from Melbourne*—but the thoughts are wrenched from me by thoughts now of her, of the actors, of the airconditioned Transit van and the cool church hall. Why didn't I go with them? What was I thinking?

They're out there playing, have been playing all morning, they're free, and here am I, a prisoner, chewing my brains out, worrying, for nothing.

I go outside, I'm not sure why. It's extraordinary out there, under that sun. I start walking across the oval—way off over in the distance I can see the vague shape of a tractor working the paddocks, a cloud of dust rising, drifting and overtaking it, pushed by a faint, barely detectable breeze. Out in the centre of the oval, where all the meals are served, signs of our occupation are clear. There is no grass out there now, just trampled earth, the concrete cricket pitch is stained with the grease leached from fallen food, small chicken and chop bones lie scattered in the dirt, a couple of screwed-up paper towels are waiting to be carried off by the wind. I stop there in the centre of the oval for a moment but then as I do I become aware that behind the curtains of all these caravans other writers' eyes must be watching. I'm not supposed to be out here; I'm supposed to be working. In my head I make up an excuse: I'm going to see Georg Büchner's garden. But I don't know where Georg Büchner lives. The caravans are arrayed in a circle around me, there are probably about fifty in all, but I don't know which one is Büchner's.

Are you coming over to help with the lunch? says a voice behind me. Yes, I say, turning around. It's Jane

Austen, the redhead, in a pale blue cotton dress with a straw hat on her head. I'm Jane, she says *(But you can't be, I think)*, are you coming over? Yes, I say. We start walking. How is your work going? she asks. I don't know what to say. I find it hard to work in the afternoon, she says—does your caravan get hot too? Yes, I say. We walk in silence. Every moment, every day, another thing to make me think this is not of this world. I'm Wayne, I say. She smiles. Under a tap at the corner of the changing shed a young woman in overalls with a purple headscarf holding back a tangle of black curls is washing out a paintbrush. The mix of paint and water has formed a little red river, running across the concrete slab and down onto the gravel. How's it going? asks Jane Austen. Good, says the young woman with the headscarf: come and have a look. This is Wayne, says Jane Austen. I'm Trish, says Trish. We go around the back; all the painters are there, with brushes and rollers in their hands, all dressed in old oversized shirts or overalls, all with some kind of hat on their heads. They're all standing back, looking at their mural, which now Jane Austen, Trish and I are looking at too.

It's a community mural. It depicts the community. There's a farmer holding a sheaf of wheat, a farmer riding a tractor, a farmer's wife holding a cake, throwing back her head and laughing; there's a big truck and a receding road, children running a footrace, a football player flying for a mark. But my eye is drawn most strongly to the man in the bottom right-hand corner holding in his outstretched arms a piebald calf. It's the caretaker from the church. He doesn't look happy, and this unhappiness—or better, disquiet—has been captured perfectly by the painter. With a few rough brushstrokes the whole broken life is revealed. What do you think? says Trish, beside me. It's done from photographs? I ask. Yes, she says. I love it, says Jane. Did they pose? I ask. Some did, says Trish. We've tried not to glamorise things too much, says another voice beside me, which on turning I see is the voice of the woman with the hennaed hair I saw—when was it? yesterday? the day before? She has a chain with trinkets around her neck—there are wrinkles there, and sunspots—she must be about fifty. The idea is to try to capture the community in time, she says, and to give it a sense of continuity and belonging. But it's not even disquiet, I think, as I look at the brushstrokes of the caretaker's face; it's humiliation. He looks humiliated. Then I look at his shoes; they're not farmers' boots, they're black vinyl slip-ons.

I keep staring at the mural, the sun burning my neck, but now around me everyone has started to move away. The dirty brushes are dropped into a bucket; they all take off their over-shirts and overalls and put them into a big khaki canvas bag. The lids of the paint tins are tapped down tight and carried two by two to the henna-headed woman's old HiAce, parked a little way off with its back door raised. There's a strong sense of camaraderie, a jokey rapport, between all the painters; they're like happy workers in an old-fashioned movie. Jane Austen and I can only watch. Are you coming in to help now? she says.

It only strikes me once I'm inside the kitchen-cum-storage area, with its concrete floor and grey metal shelves and stacks of tables and chairs, how this part of the building actually fits into the whole. Essentially, the changing shed is divided into three parts: the home team's changing room at one end, the opposition's at the other, and a storage area in the middle. I've entered the storage area through a door in the back wall on which the mural is being painted; now, to my right, on the other side of the brick wall, is the men's (home team's) showers and toilets and to my left the women's (opposition's). At the far end of the storage area I can see the door to the little kiosk out the front from where pies, tea, coffee and sweets would be served during the season.

The lunch detail has already started; there are about a dozen people inside. The trestle tables and plastic chairs are being carried out; from the grey metal shelves big boxes marked CUTLERY, CROCKERY, CONDIMENTS,

TABLECLOTHS are being handed down and carried outside. I join the workers at the far end of the room and alongside Jane Austen take the loaves of white bread from the racks in the corner and at a trestle table near the fridge start buttering slices of it. I'm feeling useful. Others join us at the table—a musician and two painters—we're all wearing surgical gloves and soon we have a system going: I butter the bread and hand it to the musician who adds a slice of cheese, the first painter then adds two slices of tomato and hands it on to his fellow painter who then sprinkles it with salt and pepper before handing it to Jane Austen who puts a buttered piece of bread on top, slices the sandwich diagonally and stacks it onto a tray. When the tray is full another artist takes it away and puts an empty one in its place. Other artists are getting large jugs of orange cordial from the fridge and carrying long tubes of white plastic cups outside. With a tray of sandwiches I move outside too. The tables have been set up in the centre of the oval, under a blazing sun. I sit beside Jane Austen who sits next to the painter Trish with the henna-headed woman alongside her. Some of the other painters come over and take their seats, then the writers and musicians start drifting over and take what seats are left.

Now Polly appears—from out of nowhere it seems. She starts chatting to someone, idly picking up and eating a sandwich as she does. I watch her, I can't help it. She catches my eye, then turns away—but then she looks back at me again. Now I turn away, pretending to look elsewhere—but I can't turn away for long. I look back—now she is looking away. Then she glances back to see if I am looking. I feel sick, nauseous, right down in the pit of my stomach. I look down at my white-bread cheese and tomato sandwich and everything turns vivid white. I can feel Jane Austen looking at me but I can't look back at her. I push my chair back and stand up. I try to catch my breath. I need to take some lunch back to Gwen, I say. But my voice has barely gone above a whisper. I pick up the plate with the sandwich on it, the plastic cup of cordial, and push my way past the chairs.

Everything is white, blazing white, there is nothing but white: the white ground, the white sky, the white plate, the white cup, the white sandwich. I can actually see a dry crust forming on the bread—all the way across the oval I hold the plate out in front of me, conscious of the eyes of all the others, watching my back, watching my progress.

Back inside the caravan, Elizabeth Jolley is asleep. She's pushed her notebook down to the end of the bed and is curled up facing the wall with the sheet drawn up to her chin. I don't know how she does it; you can feel the heat radiating down through the ceiling so strongly that, standing up, it almost burns the top of your head. I put the plate and cup on the table and lie down on the floor. It's cool down there on the lino; I lie on my back with my knees up and close my eyes. I don't know what I've done, I should have gone with the actors, now I'm stuck in a caravan with an old woman sleeping. Where my body touches the floor—my shoulder blades, my upper back, my buttocks, the soles of my feet—I let the cool seep into my skin. I want to eat the sandwich but I can't get up; thoughts, images, and sometimes thoughts and images together, float across my mind. I hear the flywire door and see a shape above me. It's Polly. She's come to see if I'm okay. I have trouble getting up. Yes, I tell her, I am; it's probably just the heat. I've just been lying down, I say, I'm feeling better now. Her face is red, there's a thin film of sweat on her brow, her upper lip, her neck. I offer her the cup of cordial. You look thirsty, I say. I tell myself I must be careful, I must be very careful now how I look at her, but as she takes the cup from me there is something so awkward and fleshy about her that I don't know why but all of a sudden I am running one hand up her back while the other dives down the front of her dress. The table is up, we have nowhere else to go; we fuck on the floor, me steering my cock past her knickers which give way with a slight tearing sound, her lapping at my tongue, my lips, my ear. I don't even think about Elizabeth Jolley, asleep in the bunk bed above, all I am conscious of is that smell of green apples, sour-sweet and overpowering. Polly keeps lapping at me for some time after I've come, then, sensing the distance I have put between us, she pulls herself out from under me and stands up. She has a red rash around her neck and a wisp of hair across one eye. I should go now, she says. There's nothing to say. She washes her face in the sink and goes.

This encounter enlivens me, all the nausea is gone, I feel like a new man: all afternoon while Elizabeth Jolley sleeps I apply myself with renewed vigour to my story. Perhaps my decision to stay here was not such a bad one after all; perhaps something is happening now, just when I was sure it wouldn't? All the curtains are drawn, I'm in my own world; even though I know it's still hot out there I in fact feel strangely comfortable and cool. I work all afternoon: occasionally thoughts of the encounter with Polly come unbidden to my mind—the hot sweat under her breasts, the dramatic quivering of her bottom lip, the pattern of creases on the back of her dress as she goes. It's terrible, I can't help it, I shouldn't think it, I'm working hard, for myself, but every time I see these things in my mind's eye I also get the feeling that what I'm doing now, what I'm writing, is for her, for Polly, that our fuck was some kind of contract we have entered into, and that the onus is now on me to deliver. I *want* to think I'm free— even now, *now*—but I'm not. *Perhaps everything I do is for Polly*—she's given me my topic, a place to work, the warm comfort of her loins. And once thinking these things I find it hard to think anything else: that we make our art here, for example, in the spirit of independence, that we are somehow ungoverned, that our lives and our works are our own. No, from the moment we stepped up into our caravans, we have all been paying off a debt.

At some point midway through the afternoon I run out of paper—I go to the end of Elizabeth Jolley's bunk and steal a few sheets from her notepad. She has written almost nothing, the scratching of her pen was the sound of her doodling, crude amateurish drawings for a story she still hasn't written. I look at her sleeping, her shallow breathing—how long has she been sleeping now?

It's late in the day when I look up from my work and see the new commotion outside. The tents have arrived. Workers I've not seen before are unloading them off the back of a tray truck and dumping them on the gravel near the changing shed. Under Polly's supervision a band of volunteers is carting them out through the players' gate onto the oval. They start going up, some easier than others, all different shapes and sizes—small silver two-man dome tents, big green canvas ones. Is it dinner? asks Gwen. I tell her no, it's still afternoon, but the tents have arrived, they're going up now. Soon you'll be rid of me, she says. She sinks back into the pillows. Are you all right? I ask. It's my stomach, she says, I'm getting these terrible pains. Can I get you something? I ask. No, she says, it will pass. I look out the window again. Half a dozen tents have gone up now; they're lining them up in an arc, with the flaps facing in towards the centre of the oval. One of the painters—the swarthy one with dreadlocks who put the cheese on the sandwiches—stands jokingly in front of one of them like a proud home-owner, arms akimbo, while another painter pretends to take his picture. They're having fun. I look down at my papers spread out on the table—*but in July when the ground was sodden and the raindrops fell like heavy jewels from the trees there was little they could do but retreat inside the single-room hut and sit by a smouldering fire*—then out the window again. Even from this distance I can feel Polly's frenetic energy: the tents have arrived, life is chaos, there is so much to do.

The tray truck drops the last of the tent rolls and moves away—at the same time I see the Transit van returning: the two vehicles pass each other going in opposite directions and now the old HiAce starts up and follows the tray truck out. I see the actors getting out of the Transit van, in particular the actor called Marti—she is wearing a lurid pink skirt and yellow socks and is jumping around gesticulating madly. Now a dark blue late-model Ford sedan appears—the procession is endless—it turns onto the gravel track and drives slowly around to the changing shed which I now see has been hung with bunting and flanked by colourful silk flags on the end of bamboo poles. I see the painters, adding the finishing touches, and the actors milling around. I see Polly come flapping towards them and put them to work—two by two the actors pick up a tent and cart it out onto the oval. The dark blue Ford sedan stops beside the changing shed and a woman gets out of the passenger seat. Shouldn't you go out there and help them? asks Gwen, peeking out the top bunk window. They're nearly finished, I say, are you still in pain? A little, she says. Stupid situation. I start counting the tents but have only got to eighteen when she, my partner, is at the door. Thirty tents, she says, how many more people is that, do you think? I've only begun to think through my answer when she changes the subject again: Did you know the Arts Minister is here? She's standing above me now. No, I say. She holds my head in her hands and kisses it, as if I were a little child. So how was your day?

she asks. What can I say?—I fucked Polly, like an animal, on the floor here—but before I've had a chance to speak she is speaking to Elizabeth Jolley: And what about you, Gwen? Gwen says she's not feeling well. My partner moves up closer to her and they start talking in hushed voices: Gwen is telling her her problems, my partner listens seriously; I hear the words 'reflux' and 'tension' but then they both lower their voices even further and I hear nothing but a monotonous murmur.

I put away my papers. How many more days like this? I get fed, yes, but really, in the end, is it all worth it? In my mind's eye I see the tray truck driving away, the two workers in the front seat: the radio is on, one of them has left half a doughnut in a white paper bag on the dashboard and he now takes it out and eats it. On the passenger side floor there's an empty Coke can, a scuffed copy of this morning's paper and a silver thermos flask that keeps rolling from side to side. They look out the windscreen through the two clean arcs the wipers have made. For hours this morning they drove all over the city, stopping late at a milk bar to get some sausage rolls and doughnuts, picking up the tents—two here, five there, some from houses, some from second-hand dealers, some from a warehouse that a man in blue jeans and a black t-shirt opened for them—then, after a lunch of pies and chocolate bars at a roadside takeaway just before the freeway, they took the road to H——.

Are you coming out? she says: I'm on dinner duty, we're doing a performance later. I tell her I'll be there soon. I watch the light outside slowly change. Another day. Are you all right? asks Elizabeth Jolley. Yes, I say. Then: Do you think this is right, all this? There's a long silence from up on the bunk. Is there somewhere else you'd rather be? she asks. Obviously, I answer. There's another pause. But then the pause goes on. No, she's not going to reply. I get up from the table and go outside.

five

Dinner is cold chicken and salad, and the usual casks of red and white wine. I pick at my meal, seated between Jane Austen and an older male painter who keeps talking to me about horizon lines and the overwhelming sky. When most people have finished their meals and are looking around for dessert, Polly stands up at the end of the table. She has changed from the clothes she was wearing earlier in the day *(Does she shower with the other women?)* and is now wearing a close-fitting black dress and big silver earrings. Beside her at the head of the table is the woman who got out of the dark blue sedan. Someone holds up a candlestick, lighting them both, and there is a spontaneous round of applause. Polly holds up two flattened palms and pushes them out in short shoving movements as if pushing the praise away from her. The applause dwindles. Polly smiles. Thank you, she says. She's got that red rash on her neck again. Goodness me, she says. The old painter next to me leans over and whispers, so close I can smell the red wine on his breath: She's a bit of a spunk, really, isn't she? I smile like I'm grimacing and nod my head like a horse.

Polly is speaking. A couple of things first, she says. She tells us about the hot water, which has been running out. Please restrict your showers to three minutes, she says. Now she's talking about the tents. You may have noticed, she says, that today our artists' camp has expanded substantially, with the addition of thirty new dwellings of various sizes. Some of us look around; the tents have formed a small camp now within the larger settlement, arrayed in a crescent from the players' gate to just past the half-forward flank at the main road end. They all stand solemnly, their flaps zipped shut. Things are beginning to happen, says Polly, glowing, and I'd like to take this opportunity now to thank you all for your patience. Some really wonderful work is being done, work of which we can all, collectively, be very proud. There will be some quite major changes taking place within the coming days but the first thing I should say is that we will soon be taking delivery of a substantial quantity of new arrivals, writers mostly—arrangements for their receival I will outline in a moment. Also—could you hold that light a little higher? Yes—as I have already mentioned to some of you we are this evening honoured by a visit from the State Minister for the Arts, who also has an important announcement to make. Some people applaud, but many don't, unsure whether or not this is cause for celebration. I think you would agree, Polly continues, perhaps to clarify the situation for us, that this visit from such an important government representative indicates to a very great degree the high cultural and economic value placed on this project *(Project?)* at the very senior levels of government. The Minister nods and smiles. Everyone goes quiet. Polly's face flickers on and off. Now, everyone, please, she says—suddenly, as if prodded—raise your cups! I want to toast the actors! Everyone raises their cups. Andrew gets up and walks to the end of the table next to Polly. To the actors! says Polly. To the actors! says everyone. Polly steps back, looks at her notes and takes a long sip of wine. The candlestick is moved in front of Andrew—he tightens his cheekbones and steels his jaw. Thanks Polly, he says.

I feel like I'm going to be sick. I nudge the old painter next to me and point to the cask of red wine. He hands it down the table to me; I fill my cup and drink. The stars are out, it's a hot summer's evening, beneath our feet an orchestra of crickets; someone's left the light on in their caravan and an eerie drift of yellow light falls out onto the grass. It's such a big universe, and we are so embarrassingly small. As you'd probably be aware, Andrew is saying, if you've seen the flyers in the toilets, we'll soon be giving you a short performance of a work-in-progress. But, and this is what Polly's talking about, behind the scenes our troupe has also been working very hard to secure our financial and artistic independence. He grins. Well, I'm happy to say that things have moved surprisingly quickly. With Polly's help and with a bit of good old-fashioned hard work we have been able to secure for the troupe a tour that will involve playing up to two shows a day in schools and community centres in towns throughout the region. In this way, we have ensured our financial independence—and, as I'm sure everyone here knows, without financial independence you cannot have artistic independence: the two are inextricably linked. So, says Andrew, with the body language of a man whose future is assured: that's all for now, but stay tuned for further developments! Everyone laughs, and gives Andrew a big round of applause. Polly steps back into the light—there's more good news to come and we listen to her detailing of it. She is happy to announce that after long negotiations with the shire council our visual arts coordinator has secured permission for our painters to paint a large mural—the largest mural in the Southern Hemisphere, she says—on one of the wheat silos in town, celebrating the working life of the local farming community. This is a major project, says Polly, a major, major project, and one that has secured the full backing of the local community: the shire believes this mural has the potential to become a major tourist attraction and ultimately to provide significant economic input into the town. Congratulations, Liz, congratulations, painters! All the cups are raised again. It's getting tedious. The string quartet has got work playing lunchtime concerts at old people's homes. The writers, she is saying—but I'm not listening—the writers, unfortunately she is saying—I'm undressing her, from the shoulders first, then the zip at the back, peeling it down, her red lace bra, the rib cage and stomach—are proving to be a problem and we as yet, she is saying, have no solution in the short to medium term. I've got the dress down to her ankles now, she stands feet together, red bra and knickers—but then all of a sudden everyone is clapping, Polly has stopped speaking, people are filling their cups, everyone is talking, the actors are all getting up from their seats and moving away. The red wine is going straight to my head. I look around: across the table Oscar Wilde and Sylvia Plath are quietly talking, down the table a little way Trish has her arm draped around the neck of the painter with dreadlocks, out over on the edge of the dull yellow circle of candlelight a small dog is crunching a chicken bone that a young child is trying to pull from its mouth. Is that my place, my only place, back there at the drop-down table with Elizabeth Jolley up on the bunk?

Now Polly is calling out, loudly, almost hysterically. Everyone! Everyone! she says. She's sweeping us towards her with her arms. Bring your chairs! she says. People start picking up their chairs and moving across the oval to the changing shed. I fill my cup again. The Transit van's headlights go on and it is gradually manoeuvred, backwards and forwards, until it is lighting the front wall of the changing shed where the actors are setting their props. I see the table, the telephone. Andrew gets out of the Transit van and starts pointing directions. Polly is still shouting. I pick up my chair, and the cask of red wine.

The Arts Minister is a shortish woman, probably in her early fifties. She's wearing a loose-fitting white summer dress and white fashionable-looking sandals. She gives the distinct impression, as Polly subtly moves her into the light on the gravel rise in front of the kiosk window, of having just come from her hotel room where after a quick shower she has drunk two glasses of crisp white wine while looking through the notes her personal assistant has given her and catching glimpses of the evening news on the television in the corner. She's on a whirlwind tour of the region; tomorrow she will be visiting a craft gallery in a town somewhere further north. Her shoulders are pink with sunburn; her hair is slightly wet. People have started setting their chairs in rows a few metres in from the boundary fence, with a view of the gravel rise and the shed wall. I sit up the back and off to one side. Polly waits for everyone to settle, the minister is looking through her notes, behind them both a couple of actors are hanging a painted backdrop—the top corners tied by lengths of twine to the downpipes at either end of the shed—showing the internal wall of an office, with a view through the window of an abstract city skyline. One of the painters must have done it. The actors exit stage left and right. Polly coughs and smiles stupidly. The minister's driver gets out of his car and leans on the boundary fence.

Thank you, says Polly, your attention please. Another speech—I will not undress her this time. I listen closely, telling myself this is all very important, that my position is precarious, that I need to take things much more seriously from now on. The Arts Minister is introduced: we appreciate that her time is valuable, her support is greatly appreciated, such initiatives as these are always fraught in the beginning but must be given time to grow. We have all been very busy, we are told, our acting group especially— they will soon give a short performance for us. I fill my cup from the cask. We believe, Polly is saying, we believe, she says, that we have achieved some wonderful things in the short time we have been together but equally we believe that there are many great things still to be achieved. There's an uncoordinated smattering of applause. Polly steps aside, literally steps sideways like a crab, and introduces the minister—she then places her clasped hands over her pubis and dashes her eyes around. The minister takes Polly's spot. She glances at her notes. Thank you, Polly, she says. There's a strange radiance coming off the minister, almost all the actors who have been standing off to one side now have their hands clasped like Polly and many in the audience sit forward in their chairs and subtly straighten their spines.

First of all, says the minister, I want to thank you all for inviting me here this evening. This stop was originally not on my itinerary, I was on my way straight through to Mildura. But before I begin (she lowers the hand with the notes in it as if it has become momentarily redundant), can I just take this opportunity to thank Polly here for all the wonderful work she has done in setting this project up? (Some people start applauding—but the minister is speaking again.) We have, she says, as I understand it, had our fair share of teething problems and it seems Polly has handled it all like a true professional. Thank you, Polly.

(Now everyone applauds properly. Polly nods and smiles. The applause stops. The minister raises the hand with the notes in it and continues.) The arts play a vital role in the life of any nation—from the writer in his or her garret to the community arts worker helping the local schoolchildren with their mosaics. Without art and the artists who make it, we are impoverished as a people. This acceptance of the arts by all strata of society as a thing integral to its proper workings has now become a commonplace. Many, many members of our communities, both young and old, people who perhaps twenty years ago would not have had the opportunity to engage with the arts, are now artists themselves of one kind or another and in turn are bringing a new generation of artists along with them. This is a very exciting time. The arts have begun to find their way into almost every aspect of our lives; in the city, where I think most if not all of you are originally from, in the city, as you know, we see this artistic sea change manifesting itself in the architecture, the streetscapes, the bohemian café life, the plethora of festivals, the number of galleries, poetry readings, performances, recitals—from being a society undernourished and enervated we have become one that now feeds gluttonously on every aspect of arts practice. You all, in your various submissions to both state and federal funding bodies, have already demonstrated the almost incomprehensible variety of projects that are being dreamed up in the wake of this enormous release of creative energy. Nothing is impossible—a dictum which this particular project has already proved. But, unfortunately, it is one thing to speak of the riches of a city's cultural life and another to speak of the countryside's impoverishment. People on the land are doing it hard: natural disasters, tough international markets, soil degradation, the impact of unemployment and a new generation of disaffected, alienated youth—and yet, again, where we see community and cultural fragmentation, ennui, spiritual vacuity, we again see the role the arts can play in recovering self-esteem, regaining confidence, rebuilding community, restoring employment and reinvigorating economic activity. It is my and my government's belief that such a role is the role the arts can and should play. I see this project as a blueprint for a new way forward, where the bridges are built between city and bush, where governments and communities become 'inclusive' rather than 'exclusive', where the arts are seen not as an 'add-on' but a vital link in the societal chain. I am not a lone voice in this, my view is shared by many others in Cabinet— the Premier himself is following this project with a great deal of interest and has promised to pay a visit personally in the very near future. In the meantime—Polly?—in the meantime it is my very great pleasure to announce that in recognition of the faith the government has in the future health of this project I will now hand over a cheque for the full purchase price, as negotiated with its owners, of the church hall in town, which will now become the permanent home, with provision for office and rehearsal space, of the 'New Directions' theatre group.

I see the cheque being handed over and I hear the very loud applause but the trouble is I haven't been listening to a word she's said. I couldn't help it, I didn't mean to, but one by one in my mind's eye I started undoing the buttons down the front of her dress. At the third button I stopped and thought for a moment about what I was doing—this was the Minister for the Arts, after all—but then, I couldn't help it, I was plunging one hand through the gap, under the cup of her bra, and with that hand I was kneading a breast that while not firm rolled and floated sensuously under my fingers. In an instant we were in the back seat of her government car—the driver like one of those servant-drivers in the movies looked out professionally through the windscreen—and I was on top of her, her dress up and her legs wrapped around me and me pounding myself into her. Her eyes are closed, she's giving herself savagely to me, I with each manly thrust inveigle myself more and more into this horrible, perverse, unhealthy contract. She is saying: Fuck me; I am saying: I am—and with that we wrap ourselves into a bargain more degraded than Faust's. I fuck her so hard I want her to bleed, she gasps so badly it sounds like she might choke. She knows how sick and sorry this whole business is, and now she's giving herself over to it—I'll have these people pleasure me, she says, and in return I'll give them money. She grabs me by the hair and shoves my face between her legs—I do everything she tells me. Polly watches through the steam-shrouded window, running a tongue across her lips.

I've not quite reached the end of this daydream— the minister has not quite got what she wanted—when I realise things have moved rapidly on. The minister has taken a seat down in the front row—I can just see the back of her head—and the performance is already well under way. With big gestures and loud voices two of the actors are settling an argument as to who should be the first through an imaginary door. All the audience are laughing; I laugh too. Then there's the scene with the table and the telephone, just like back at the hall, then the park, her as a dog, then someone who I think is the garbage man, then the office again, and an argument between two people. Then finally she comes bounding back on as the dog—the audience go into hysterics, they start applauding, whistling—then she steps up out of being a dog to address us and particularly the minister directly. She is doing an epilogue, she's no longer a dog but an actor, in iambic pentameter the minister is thanked and everyone applauds.

The show is over, things quieten down; people mill around the minister almost as if they might expect her to start signing autographs. I push my way forward so as to study her at closer range: her foundation has been applied unevenly and one cheek is paler than the other; around the rims of her nostrils the skin is very pink, almost red; there's a blue biro mark on her arm. The actors are taking down the backdrop and putting away the props—the minister walks over to them and shakes all their hands in turn: a few words are exchanged, there's a burst of laughter, then accompanied by Polly the minister returns to her car where the driver is already in the front seat, waiting. Out on the oval people are clearing the trestle tables and putting things into boxes, others are carting the cleared tables away, still others are stacking the chairs. The lights start going on in some of the caravans, some people are already moving to the showers with their towels slung over their shoulders. Polly and the minister have one last chat before the minister's car pulls away. It drives off around the gravel track; then, like a continuation of the merry-go-round, another set of headlights approaches. These ones are very bright and very wide apart. Another pair follows the first, then another pair after that. They're buses, big touring coaches; they move slowly around the gravel track towards the changing shed: the air brakes hiss, the cloud of dust settles, the doors fold back, and the drivers get out.

Polly hasn't moved—she has said goodbye to the minister and now she is welcoming the buses. We've all stopped what we're doing to stand and look. Dull lights are on inside them and you can see the faces peering out, some with their hands cupped to the windows. Polly and the three drivers gather near the front of the first bus: I can see the drivers handing over their paperwork and Polly checking through it and signing it where needed. She steps up into each bus in turn and gives a short, presumably welcoming, speech, then steps down from the last bus and starts giving shouted instructions to us: our new guests have arrived, they'll need to be fed, can we bring the things back out, please? No-one is particularly keen to do what Polly says—we've had enough, had enough of it all, we want to go back to our vans, but one by one we relent and start setting up for dinner again.

The new arrivals get down from the buses and gather on the other side of the boundary fence. Polly is giving them an overview of the camp, pointing variously at the tents, the changing shed and the centre of the oval where the trestle tables are going up again. I watch all this, I have not moved, I am standing just inside the fence, with the cask of red wine in one hand and the plastic cup in the other. More writers: they stream out of the buses and mill around in a mass. Polly moves around the edge of this mass like a sheepdog, trimming a corner here, a corner there, moving the whole thing slightly in one direction, then the other. She herds them through the players' gate out onto the oval towards the tables. I retreat to my van. It's all too much. Elizabeth Jolley has the light on and is working up on the bunk. More writers, I say. She doesn't look up. I sit at the table and drink the wine. More writers.

My partner comes home—she looks scornfully at the wine and even more scornfully at me. Do you have anything to say? she asks. I look up at her, my head wobbling involuntarily on the top of my neck. That's good news about the hall, I say. She sits down opposite me and lowers her voice. It takes a while to gain eye contact with me. Things are going to be very different from now on, she is saying: I'm going to be away a lot of the time, I think you've got to be careful of getting stuck in a rut here, of seeing everything so negatively. You've got to apply your-self, show a bit of initiative—there *is* a way out if you're prepared to take it. She pauses. I drink. I'm annoyed with you for what you did, she says, that was a golden opportunity, working with us, you only had to take it. Now look at you. She's talking about the dramaturgy. I'm working on my Laburnum story, I say, it's going well; you'll see. She's not convinced. You're so negative, she says, you see this whole thing as if it's some kind of evil scheme with some awful ulterior motive, as if they're out to get us—for what? They're trying to help us; isn't that obvious? I look at her: she's happy, she's radiant, she has a theatre troupe, they have a home, they're going to be touring the land. I'm sorry, I say. You shouldn't drink so much, she says. She's right. You're right, I say. I stand up, steadying myself on the table. I'll take it back, I say, meaning the cask. She shakes her head, in pity, I think. I'm sorry, I say, really, it's just I'm having trouble adjusting to all these changes. Do you remember the backyard, sitting out there in the sun? The cat on the concrete, the jasmine on the shed? I lower my voice—I know Gwen is listening. I miss all that, I hiss, why did it have to change? I don't want to live here with all these people. I want to go back to Eden, just you and me, before this.

Confident that I have left a strong impression behind, I step outside into the night. It's still very warm out there. At the tables in the centre of the oval the new arrivals are eating their dinner. There must be about a hundred of them: the atmosphere is very subdued, almost hushed; you can hear the cutlery clinking. I can't see Polly—all the others, too, have gone inside. I give the dinner tables a wide berth on my way around to the changing shed. The storeroom door is open: I take the cask inside and put it on the shelf with the others.

Then I see that at the far end of the room a light has been left on—it's not until I move closer that I see it is the light coming from under a door, a door I'd not seen before, tucked up in the far left-hand corner of the storage area and obviously leading to another smaller, perhaps more secure room behind. I push the door open: Polly is in there, sitting at a desk with her back to me. The room is tiny, ridiculously tiny. Along one wall is a narrow bed, tucked under shelves groaning with boxes of papers and other paraphernalia. Other boxes are piled up on the floor and on top of the cupboard against the opposite wall. It is Polly's home, her sleeping quarters and office—this is where she's been living. I'm looking at the back of her head, I don't think she's heard me come in, but then out of the blue she is talking—to me, I presume. I understand your feelings, she is saying, I'm sympathetic to your situation, really I am, but you must try and see it from my point of view. She turns around—then, at the same time, from behind the door I have just opened onto him, the caretaker steps forward. He's been talking to Polly; Polly was answering him, not me. Now she sees me standing in the doorway—we are standing together, the caretaker and I—but after a flicker of recognition she decides to treat me as if I'm not there, or if I am, that it doesn't bother her, in fact she welcomes the audience, let them all come in, the more the merrier, let them all come in and see what she's being made to put up with—if the rest of the camp suddenly started crowding into the doorway I don't think she could have been happier. You've got no idea, she is saying to the caretaker: I've just taken delivery of eighty-six new writers, most of them straight out of their courses, and there are another two busloads arriving tomorrow. It's not up to me, she says, very firmly, very directly, it's not up to me to decide whether the overall aims of this scheme are being achieved—it's enough for me just coping with the outrageous quantity of artists that I'm now supposed to house and feed. I don't know what it's doing for your town—to be honest I don't care. As it is I am stretching the paltriest resources as thin as I possibly can to accommodate a group of people who in my opinion might be much better off left fending for themselves. Polly falls back into her chair and gulps something from a plastic cup. She looks terrible, her hair is all askew. What are you doing here, anyway? she asks.

I'm not sure what to say. I point behind me to indicate where I have just put the wine cask, thinking perhaps I should tell her how I have brought it back and why—that I'm going to be more sensible from now on, harder working, more responsible—but it would take too long to explain. Instead I say: I wanted to ask when the old lady might get a place of her own? Polly looks at me condescendingly and drinks her whisky. She then tops it up from the bottle on the floor beside her. She is about to speak, but the caretaker, who has been jiggling his hands nervously in his pockets all this time, cuts in. I was here first, he says. He steps forward a little, deliberately putting me to his rear. I don't actually care if the hall is sold or rented, he is saying—completely ignoring me and speaking directly and very forcefully to Polly—whether we own it or you own it: that's not my point. The point is, that according to your propaganda, this whole scheme is supposed to be fixing our problems for us. But now if this Andrew bloke turns around like he did today and tells me that he won't be needing me any more to look after the hall because, I don't know, because they're too good for that, well, I can't see how exactly that is fixing anything. It's not, says Polly, with a hiss—and with that she turns her back on us: as far as she's concerned the conversation is finished. The caretaker rocks back and forth on the balls of his feet. He looks at me angrily—where did I come from? What's it got to do with me? Then he turns and goes.

I stand there looking at the back of Polly's head. She drags another chair up beside her and gestures for me to sit. She pours whisky into two plastic cups: I take the drink and sit. I want us to forget what happened today, she says. She's talking about the fuck. I nod my head. Forgotten, I say. She allows herself some time to think. Do you think this was a good thing, she says, coming here, this change? I shrug my shoulders. We both drink. The thing is, says Polly, I'm not sure what good we're actually doing. Good? I ask. Well, says Polly, there's no question we've got all these people out of the city so the new developments can happen but now that we've got you all here—well, all right, listen. She stops, leans over, picks up one of the boxes stacked up all around us and empties the contents onto the desk. It's a big stack of papers, in bulging manila folders. Two silverfish crawl out from under the pile and run around the desk: Polly kills them with the flat of her hand and brushes them onto the floor. This, she says, lifting up the thick folders one by one and making another pile with them: this is just some of the work that has already been handed in. *(Handed in?)* All kinds of work, every style—they're waiting for it to be transferred to computer. But it won't be transferred to computer—there are no computers, as you can see. She sweeps an arm around the room. No, it will stay here in boxes like this until there is no more room for it and then it will be taken back to the city and pulped. At around this point, she says, each writer will start receiving their rejection slips from the publishers we have supposedly sent their manuscripts to—here they are, in here, all prepared, all ready to go. (She pulls open a drawer and takes out another manila folder with the words Rejection Slips scribbled on it: she opens it up and pushes some of these slips across to me.) All the usuals, as you can see—*not suited to our list, list is full*—you'll all get half a dozen each of these and that's the end of that. Some of the more deluded among you might have another go at another piece of work, some might even try for a third or fourth, but in the end you'll all be worn down. You will decide, and the quicker the better (this new young lot I hope very quickly), that this is not the life you wanted after all. You'll become copy editors or arts bureaucrats, advertising people—citizens, that is, *who might actually make a worthwhile contribution to society*. But what about Laburnum, I say, I'm making good progress—wasn't the idea that there might be a pre-existing readership for such a piece, and that once I'd written it you would help me find that readership? Where on earth did you get that idea from? she says. Here—she takes some of the rejection slips from the top of the pile—you might as well have yours now. There's a pause. She smiles. She laughs. I want to smile too—clearly it is all a big joke—but I can't. So the question is, says Polly, getting all serious again: what good are all these writers, what worthwhile contribution could any of you possibly ever make, how could any of you ever possibly pay your way?

She's serious. She's seriously looking at me. I don't know what to say. The actors have found a way, the painters, and the musicians—I thought that by writing my history of Laburnum I too was making some sort of contribution. Obviously I'm not, nor any of the others; Elizabeth Jolley sits up on her bunk all day working and what she does is utterly worthless. But don't get me wrong, Polly is saying, tomorrow I will distribute kits to each of our new arrivals—by tomorrow evening there might be ten new histories of Laburnum being written, ten new collections of poems dealing with the minutiae of domestic life, and each will then enthusiastically employ themselves on the content of these kits in the hope of making something of them. But the fact is, this work will serve no purpose, it will leave no mark, it will simply gather dust in the boxes here and get eaten by the silverfish. Yes?

There's someone at the door. It's Büchner. He's brought

another box of papers. He's the paper collector. He won't let me catch his eye. He puts the box on a stack of others and leaves the room quietly again. Polly looks at the hole he's made in the air. Anyway, she says, turning back to me: there it is. That's it. I like you. You fucked me. I feel like you should know the truth. There'll be changes tomorrow, new challenges—she's standing up, pushing in her chair, giving me the hint I should go—so let's leave what is left of this day and sleep. She grabs a linen sheet, gives it a flick, lets it rise up and settle back down softly on the bed. *(In here, I think, with no windows?)* For some time I stand and watch Polly going about her business: smoothing the sheet with her hand, fluffing the pillow, taking her pyjamas out from under it and fluffing it up again. She unzips her dress. She stands and looks at me. I realise I am meant to go. Close the door behind you, she says.

Outside it's very warm, very still; the air is heavy, loaded. The deep black sky, the number of stars—these are things that cannot be described. The camp is quiet. Here and there a light is on, in the tents torches and candles eerily flicker. A small group of new writers are sitting in a circle of chairs outside one of them, leaning forward and talking quietly together, no doubt trying to make sense of the situation they've found themselves in. I should tell them not to bother.

I can hear a tap running—from the tap on the shed wall beside me where earlier in the day the brushes were washed I follow the snaking line of a hose until my eye arrives at Büchner's caravan. The light is on inside, I can just make out the shape of George Bernard Shaw at the table, and in the light spilling out into his garden—low shrubs, herbs, flowers—the shape of Georg Büchner with a hose in his hand.

PART TWO

one

Light rain is falling, you can hear the water dripping from
the roof. People are moving in and out under the tarpaulins with their plates of scrambled eggs, walking them
back to their caravans and tents. Old planks and other bits
of timber, in places whole pallets, have been set down over
the mud; they form an odd network of interconnecting
pathways, along which, especially now, at meal times, the
human traffic passes back and forth. The sky is leaden;
it won't rain properly, only these soft misty showers that
start, stop, and start again. A small detail has been set to
work digging trenches around the tents but a heavy shower
looks unlikely. It's not cold, in fact it's surprisingly mild—
spring is with us again and the days are getting warm.

Do you want the rest of this? asks Elizabeth Jolley
from up on the bunk. She's only taken a couple of

mouthfuls from her breakfast: Büchner takes the plate from her, sits back down at the table, pushes aside his empty plate and starts eating what is left. Gwen sinks back into the pillows. I hear a cough, then a sigh, then silence. Some days she does a little work, propped up on her pillows in the tiny sliver of weak sun falling in through the window beside her, but mostly when collection time comes Judd finds her empty-handed. The town doctor comes to visit, an urbane young man with a gentle manner: he stands next to her bunk so that he is looking her straight in the eye and they talk in low whispers; I hear her roll over, then roll back again; I hear him tapping her chest and back, pumping up the blood pressure armband and the sound of the velcro tearing. It is left to me to make sure the tablets are administered correctly.

I watch Büchner shovelling the scrambled eggs into his slack, fleshy mouth. It's funny, I've got strangely used to him since he moved in: his clumsy, fumbling ways. He'd barely got his garden going before his old housemate passed away; his caravan was repossessed and filled with five young poets, and the ruined garden with a cluster of annexes and tents. He sleeps on the bunk below Elizabeth Jolley. It's an awkward but not impossible arrangement. My partner comes back every week or so from her touring but she usually only stays one night before they are all off again somewhere else. We sleep together on the lowered-down table-bed but we know that any real intimacy is out of the question—a caravan shared with two other writers is no place for noisy lovemaking.

Each day I take my papers and go and sit out under the tree, the big old gum beside the gravel track on the right half-forward flank at the main road end. I take a chair from the storeroom, my information pack, some blank paper and a pen and under its broad canopy I make a kind of garret *en plein air*. It is a small world, the bark at my back, the gravel at my feet, the papers on my lap, the roof of branches overhead. Life in the camp—the bustling, seething life in the camp—goes on around me and I watch it as you would a dream. Smoky fires burn here and there, people move about between the dwellings; everything is painted in muted tones. Laburnum is for me now, and me alone. I know perfectly well what its fate will be, I know there is no open-plan office full of straight-backed typists transcribing my work and preparing it for publication. I write the papers, I let them go, and the next day I write some more. Once they have passed from my hands into Judd's (Büchner no longer collects them, he fell badly out of favour—but it would take too long to explain) and from there into the big blue wheelie bin with the padlocked lid that appeared at the back of the changing shed a few weeks ago (they go in there, I know they do), there is no point dwelling on them any more. It's like I told her theatre should be: I live in the moment, then the one after that.

When with wrinkled hands May Fairweather lifted from the washtub the heavy clothes and looked out the window towards the back track and saw the horse and dray approaching through the trees, her first thoughts were of her husband, who had that morning left to take their cow to market and who was not expected back till evening. May shook the water from her hands and wiped them on her apron and brushed aside a fallen lock of hair. She had just that morning been wondering again why so few people passed this way. It was not as if they still lived in complete isolation, far from all civilised society. The eastern corridor had begun to open up, acre by acre the rough bush was being cleared and tracks were being carved through it. On his infrequent visits to market Ernest Fairweather inevitably came back with another report of the extent to which the landscape had already changed—there was even talk of a rail-line coming their way, he said, even to their front door. With these thoughts in her head, May Fairweather watched the dray approaching.

Look at them all, says Büchner, pointing out the window. It's true, it's an extraordinary sight. There are almost three hundred of them now, going in and coming out of their caravans and tents, standing in groups under the plastic sheets and tarpaulins, queuing down the street for the last of the scrambled eggs. I don't know where they all come from, I don't know where they all go: somewhere up at the headwaters of writing new blood pours down every day like rain, gushing and rushing downstream until our dam is ready to burst. To see yourself as part of a community is one thing, to see yourself as part of a plague quite another. Is that what day by day makes Polly's ragged, desperate look even worse? Did she have any idea what she was letting herself in for, had anyone warned her how many people now actually call themselves, *shamelessly* call themselves, writers? She can tick the boxes and take the kudos for the acting troupe, the painted silo, the string quartet playing lunchtimes for the toothless elderly—they've gone now, the other artists, they're all out there working—but she can't get around the fact that for every writer placed, ten misplaced remain.

Polly. It's her eyes now that get to me. They have a hunted look. When on the narrow bed in her office I sink myself into her and look into her eyes for the code to her thoughts I see someone hunted—looking,

127

listening—taking pleasure in the deep sucking pull in her groin but at any moment ready for the knock at the door. Sometimes there are queues out there, snaking back through the storeroom, asking for help of some kind—they want to change their topic, there is no soap in the showers—and sometimes, yes, when we have finished our loveless lovemaking and I have dressed and opened the door they will all be standing there, all waiting their turn. She is far now from being the crisp upright sweet-sour-smelling Polly who stood at the door of the caravan in the street that day, the clipboard under her arm. All these trials have played havoc with her dress, her body, her face. She still wears the obligatory red lipstick, but she has let the other make-up go. Her skin is pasty, with a slightly sweaty sheen; she no longer wears any earrings and the holes have closed over.

Her only wish now, her only hope, is to stay on top of the numbers. It's like shovelling dry sand out of a hole. All the originals are living four, sometimes six, to the caravan (we've managed to keep our household to three, only because of our special past relationships with her); the new arrivals are crammed into the seventy or so tents and makeshift dwellings spread out all over the oval. She has acquired the adjoining paddock from the farmer who owned it and could expand the settlement out there too but she knows she will have to set limits eventually. Once you've said you will accommodate everyone—with land, housing, food, water, praise—there's no telling where it might end. Unless some kind of solution is found soon these writers will keep breeding and spreading like rabbits (or kangaroos, *passim* Büchner); they will not merely 'penetrate into the regions' but completely overrun them.

There's a big clean-out coming, says Büchner, maybe reading my thoughts. (He always has some gossip: he may have slipped down Polly's ladder but he's still good for gossip.) I saw the booking for the bus, he says, it's licensed to carry forty-two, so it looks like forty-two are going.

It happens without warning. One morning Polly comes flapping around the camp and starts rounding people up. A bus or a couple of minivans appear, the chosen writers are piled in, driven off and never heard from again. They're running workshops, Polly tells us, conducting readings, teaching courses, becoming critics, *starting careers*, and with no available evidence to the contrary we have to believe her. Jane Austen disappeared in this way, so too the writer I'd called Leo Tolstoy. Often lately they are the new arrivals—greenhorns who've barely had the chance to settle in before they are being moved on again. Sometimes there is a similarity in age, sometimes in gender, sometimes, Büchner insists, in genre or style.

But really, for all the theorising, no-one really knows why some are chosen and others not. They go from here and they never come back. They've gone to 'a better place', says Polly, a place of agents, publicists, interviews and book signings. They might get driven off a cliff for all we know. Meanwhile we stay here, in this awful slough, sucking on the dug of dubious benevolence.

Büchner picks up his plate and goes outside. The rain is clearing. Elizabeth Jolley has fallen back to sleep. It's Saturday, I should relax, pick up Laburnum on Monday. Tomorrow my partner will be home for the day; we'll go for a walk, sit together under the tree. She will ask me how it's going and I will tell her, the whole sad sorry story. Yes, I have trouble believing myself sometimes the person I am, I've become. Nights when I pound my body against my benefactress's and she talks filth into my ear it scares me to think what might become of me yet.

After lunch a football match has been organised. I go outside to watch the preparations, standing on the rise near the outer wing. Makeshift goalposts have been set up at either end of the adjoining paddock and a rough oval has been marked out with flour. Someone is picking up cow pats with a bucket and spade. A plywood score-board is propped up on two chairs with the names of the combatants on it—Poetry v Prose—and nails to hang the numbers on. It's Polly's idea of fun. Once lunch is over everyone starts moving over there, taking up their positions around the boundary line. The teams are small—like most of Polly's organised activities there is no great rush to take part. Both teams are a ragged-looking lot, indistinguishable except for the fact that all the poets are wearing hats. The crowd is enthusiastic, though, cheering and laughing as they run onto the ground.

I watch it all from my place on the rise—I've brought a chair with me and am sitting on it with a blanket over my lap. Shouts, the sound of foot on leather, the umpire's whistle, the occasional sudden uproar from the crowd, all these sounds drift to me on the still afternoon air. Over by the paddock gate a group of farmers have gathered, behind them a cluster of white utes parked at all odd angles; they are watching the game, watching us, but from a distance, so as not to interfere. Some small children run up and down the white flour boundary line, following the trajectory of the ball, back and forth, back and forth. There's a roar from the crowd and the scorekeeper hangs a '1' on the nail under 'G' next to Prose. I see Polly approaching around the gravel track from the changing shed; she walks down the grassy bank and slips under the barbed-wire fence. She's wearing her weekend clothes, jeans and a sloppy cotton top, her hair pulled back in a pony tail. The hand that feeds me. She moves around the outer edge of the crowd, some people turn and acknowledge her but no-one actually invites her into their group.

Now I see the chef approaching around the gravel track from the changing shed where a one-tonne ute is unloading supplies. He still has his apron on. He stops on the rise overlooking the paddock, bunches up the lower half of his apron and wipes his hands on it. He glances in my direction then goes back to watching the game. (We call him the chef but of course he's the caretaker. Not long after his interview with Polly she gave him the job—it's true that we had, inadvertently, taken his other one from him. With the help of usually half a dozen rostered assistants he cooks the food, morning, noon and night, to feed just under three hundred people.) I watch him standing there; then, seeing Polly, he too walks down the bank and stands at the paddock fence. He attracts Polly's attention and calls her to him. The game has tightened, Poetry has scored twice in quick succession, and the crowd around the boundary line remain oblivious to the furtive conversation now taking place between Polly and the chef. The chef points back towards the changing shed; Polly looks in that direction, then after a quick further conference she crawls back under the wire. I watch them make their way up the rise: together they walk back to the changing shed and are swallowed up in its shadow.

Is this meant to be some kind of metaphor? says Büchner, standing behind me, arms crossed, watching the game. I don't know what to say. Something's going on over there, he says, pointing back in the direction of the changing shed: they're getting something ready, just like I told you. I look back in that direction and see the ute pulling away: it drives around the gravel track, past where we are standing and out onto the road. There's a dog in the back, a backpack spray kit, some four-litre plastic poison bottles and a petrol-powered whipper-snipper. The crowd out on the paddock roars—someone has kicked a goal.

No, I don't think I'm going to do very well out of this, says Büchner, seemingly out of nowhere. Is he talking to me? He's looking out across the paddock but he doesn't seem to be watching the game. What do you mean? I say. Do you remember when you asked for the cleaning things? he says, turning to me: you too made trouble once—but you're smart, you know what side your bread's buttered on; you're fucking Polly, you're doing your work, they'll reward you in the long run. Out on the paddock a bell rings; the players and the crowd start milling around. Someone walks out with oranges on a tray; the two teams drift apart to either end of the ground where their coaches are preparing to address them. Anyway, good luck, says Büchner. He turns away. I watch him jump back across the boundary fence and disappear in among the caravans and tents. It's anyone's game, I hear the Poetry coach shouting from his huddle—he raises his volume but his next words are lost beneath the sound of his team roaring their commitment.

The third quarter is a cakewalk, by the time the bell rings for three-quarter time the result is in no doubt. I watch for another five minutes or so then pack up my things. Across the camp the shadows are lengthening, a dull sun is hanging low down in the west. A flock of white cockatoos whirls around screeching overhead then lands softly in the branches of my tree. From behind me I hear the roar of the crowd—another goal. A chill is coming down. I walk around the gravel track then jump the boundary fence and make my way along the lane between two caravans.

It's not so silly to talk of lanes now; without any particular forethought a pattern of streets, lanes and narrow pathways has developed and now separates the dwellings crammed together within the confines of the boundary fence. Some people, for a joke, have given some of them names—Hope Street, for example—and most people, with the exception of the latest arrivals, know the pattern blind. All paths lead, naturally, in some way or other, to the open area in the centre of the oval where the meals are still served and from there back to the changing shed, with its cooking, showering and toilet facilities. Here and there, at street corners, in the slip of land between two caravans, you will find small open fires surrounded by rocks or bricks, some of which are still smouldering now.

The camp is pretty well deserted, everyone seems to be out on the paddock, but as I turn from that lane into the adjacent street I see Polly, a clipboard resting on her forearm, a pen in her hand. She turns and sees me—I can hardly describe her look. Shame? She quickly scribbles something down, then turns away. Polly? I say. She half-turns towards me—her face is gaunt, hunted—and hesitates. Is she going to speak to me, tell me something that perhaps I don't want to hear? Our eyes meet only for a moment, then she turns away again. I watch her walking—fine arse!—away from me down the planks (the street) between the caravans and tents. But she only goes a little way before she stops (she knows I'm looking), checks something on her clipboard, looks at the caravan she is now facing and writes something down. Then she is off again. I watch her go—stopping, writing something down, moving on—until she turns a corner about twenty metres away and disappears from view. Is she asking me to follow her? Was that swaying arse for me? I walk a little in that direction then catch a glimpse of her again—I'm looking down the lane between two caravans and see her at the end walking past. I hurry down that lane and turn right into the lane off that one. Now I see her again, turning left. I know I am heading back towards the centre of the oval, that the trestle table area with its tarpaulin cover is ahead of me somewhere to my left, but the further I go the less certain I become. I turn again and pass between two caravans parked very close together—there is barely enough room to squeeze between them. When I emerge at the other end of this narrow lane I find myself in an open, tented area that I've never really seen before: two-man tents mostly, some in neat rows, some arranged in circles and semi-circles with their flap-doors facing inward. Now I can see Polly very clearly again, head and shoulders above the height of the tents, moving towards the arc of caravans on the other side. The small tented area I've now found myself in is not so well served with streets and paths as other parts of the camp and I have to pick my way carefully around the mud, finding only the occasional sheet of cardboard or masonite to make the going easier. But Polly is still very easy to spot, she's got her red cotton top on—a beacon in all this grey chaos and confusion. I watch her pass around the back of some tents then slip down between two caravans over near the outer wing.

When I catch up with her again it is my caravan she is standing in front of. I stand a little way off; I don't know if she's seen me. I call out to her—Polly?—but again the same routine. I approach, she moves away, stops and half looks back, then turns and walks away again. I stand, undecided—what's the point? what do I care?— then suddenly, there is Büchner. He's just stepped out of our caravan; he looks terrible, his face is all flushed, his eyes are mad and faraway, his hair hangs askew over his eyes. He has a pillow in his hands. He sees me standing, Polly walking. Shannon, I say, are you all right? He looks at me, looks through me, then again towards where Polly is disappearing. What's she doing? says Büchner. I don't know, I say. Find out, he says—was she writing down names? Hurry, now, run and catch her, he says. Why? I say—what is it this time? Büchner doesn't answer, just gives me that look. All right, I say. He goes back inside and closes the door behind him.

I search the streets and lanes for another ten minutes but I can't find Polly anywhere. I work my way back towards the changing shed—very distantly I can still hear the thump of leather and the occasional cheer from the crowd out on the paddock. The door to the storeroom and kitchen is open and the light is on inside: it's getting dark outside now and the night air is coming down. I cross the storeroom and the kitchen, now stacked high everywhere with boxes, big tins, bottles and all the other paraphernalia necessary to keep three hundred hungry writers fed. Polly's office door is open; I step inside, I don't see her at first, then suddenly she steps out from the corner behind the door and puts the clipboard on her desk. Her office is no better than the storeroom, piled high with boxes and other junk—it's just as I am thinking this that I see the new stack of four-litre plastic poison bottles against the wall beside her bed and that, simultaneously, as if reading my thoughts, Polly turns and looks at me. Her beauty was always skin deep, all surface, all hair and lipstick and clothes and tits, and now it's all wearing away and there's nothing underneath. She's like a mannequin, stripped and thrown in the corner. I feel sorry for her, deeply sorry, but feeling sorry is a long way from loving.

Polly, I say, what's going on? She looks at me—she looks weak, vulnerable, defeated—and the most fabulously filthy thoughts pass across my mind. She is about to speak, she might have spoken, but then behind me is Judd, the factotum. The game is over, he says, they need drinks. At first all I hear is 'game is over' and for a moment I think he too has entered into the spirit of this pseudo-crime-novel denouement, but then I realise he is talking about the football match: the game is over, they're waiting for drinks. I look at him: his ice-carved face, his gaunt good looks, his baggy black sweater and tight black jeans—and for a moment it becomes painfully clear to me where I stand. I see Polly bent over, me taking her from behind, but what I hear is not her moaning but the pleasure-grunts of Judd as she eagerly takes him in her mouth. I'm sorry, he says, I didn't mean to interrupt; it's just that there are a few hundred writers out there, waiting for a drink. I smile with him, or at him, I'm not sure. Polly pushes past me and follows Judd back out into the storeroom.

For a while I stand where they have left me, staring at Polly's desk, her bed, the four-litre poison bottles stacked against the wall. When I too go back out into the storeroom, Polly and Judd are gone—they've taken a stack each of wine casks and long tubes of plastic cups—and standing now at the trestle table along the wall beside the fridge, preparing what look like pastry shells, is the chef. He has his back to me, but he knows I'm there. Are you here for the shift? he says. Not really, I say. Still, you could help me anyway, couldn't you? he says, with a sly questioning tone. I join him at the table; he's covered it with flour and is rolling out small balls of pastry and shaping them into rough circles that he then presses into the little fluted aluminium pie dishes that are stacked high at the end of the table. I take over the last part of the job, pressing the pastry into the dishes. I'm not rostered on to dinner till next Thursday, but it doesn't seem to matter any more. This day is already looking like no other. We work silently like this, he flattening the dough and sliding the circle along to me, me pressing it with my fingers into the dish, and I drift off for some time into my own thoughts. It's very relaxing; there is something very comforting about working with your hands, I think, kneading dough—making clay pots might be another. Are you happy with the way things have turned out? I ask the chef, who seems also to have drifted off into his own thoughts. He looks at me a little strangely at first, then realises what I'm talking about. The job's all right, he says, but any job is better than no job at all. I'll admit it's taken a little while to get on top of things: I come from a family that wasn't that adventurous with its food—Jude herself was a meat and three veg person—so all this fancy cooking didn't come naturally to me at first. But that's the way it is—you've got to please your customers, I've learned that much at least. So with a bit of application (and a lot of work out of hours) I think I've managed to put together a pretty good menu now. Of course, it's hard to get all the ingredients—galangal I can't get for love or money—but I think that makes you more creative with your cooking in the long run. For example, that cassoulet I did last week?—I had no bay leaves, so I used a parsley substitute and I think it turned out nicely. I could do with a few more pots and pans, though, and a couple of new utensils, but you adapt your ways to suit your means. And I still get the best cuts of meat in the district, you'd have to agree with that.

I smile. There is something so soothing about what I am doing—kneading the pastry, listening to his voice, seeing his happy ending—that everything now drifts and floats and almost lets me leave my body and hover up above. The one thing I want to get on top of, though, he is saying, his voice now far away, is matching the meal with the right kind of wine. I've talked to Polly about this, he is saying, and told her that obviously the cask wine we are serving undermines everything I am trying to do as a chef and of course she's always said she'll do something about it but she never has and it looks unlikely now. I'm listening to him, I am, in fact, hearing everything he's saying, very clearly, but now that other part of me, that part outside my body, is roaming out the door across the camp. Out on the paddock it's like a big party, everyone has a white plastic cup in their hand which the appointed waiters, moving among them, fill from their casks. The red cotton top of the arts-slut Polly dashes about, telling them all how much she loves their work, and how soon, perhaps tomorrow, it will open up previously unimagined doors for them. They will be like doves released, and only from a distance will Polly see her work reflected in them. At the back of the changing shed the big blue wheelie bin is too full for the lid to close and a jumble of papers cascades from it. Judd is out there walking with his hand on Polly's arse.

So anyway, the chef is saying, wine aside, I'm making a special effort tonight. Cook something special, Polly said, and I can't tell you how many sleepless hours I've spent wondering what special might mean. And then it came to me, it's so obvious, all this effort, all this hoo-ha, all this fancy international cuisine—but what sort of meal is going to be 'special' after a game of footy on a drizzly Saturday in spring? Meat pies, mashed potatoes, carrots and peas—if Polly wanted a surprise then I imagine she's going to get it.

We finish the flans and set them aside, laid out on the trestle table in rows. The chef is stirring the big pot of meat and gravy; I set to work peeling the potatoes. It feels like we've been at it a long time but the chef assures me help will be coming soon. They're just finishing off the last of the wine, he says. The light is on in Polly's office and a white glow spills through the open doorway onto the storeroom's concrete floor. What was Büchner doing, back there in the caravan? I watch the chef stirring the big pot. He takes it off the stove. The help has still not arrived. I open the second sack of potatoes, cutting the string seam with my knife. Then I hear the hiss of air brakes outside. You can go now, says the chef.

I turn. Judd is in the doorway. Come with me, he says. I go outside. About a dozen writers are gathered around the door of a big touring bus—I recognise the faces but the funny names have all escaped me. Polly arrives, she's come from the paddock, she hasn't stopped. Now Judd hands her a big armful of manila folders and one by one Polly hands them to us. It's my Laburnum papers. The bus door hisses open; we're told to get inside. It's a big bus of the kind I remember travelling to Sydney in once a long long time ago. The lights inside are dim, there are lights embedded in the steps and in the overhead lockers; the driver watches diffidently each of our feet on the steps. There are far too few of us to fill the bus and as if by pre-arrangement we all spread out, one here, one there. I'm sitting about two thirds of the way back, on the left-hand side. I put my manila folder on the seat beside me. The last of the passengers take their seats and now I can see Polly, up the front, under the dim light, talking to the driver, her clipboard in her hand. She takes a few steps down the aisle and pointing with her forehead mentally checks us off her list. It is no accident that the last one checked is me: her look lingers, there's something strange and hard to read in her eyes—is she kissing me goodbye?—then just before she turns away I see the hint of a warm smile pass across her face. She stops again beside the driver and holds the clipboard out to him—he's signing us away—then she is down the steps and gone. The door closes with a hiss. The air brakes release, I can hear the soft clunk of the gears and the bus starts moving away.

So here I am, I'm going: it happens to us all. There is no rhyme nor reason. Even when you've sucked the fingers of the hand that feeds you it can still turn around and grab you by the throat. Of course I'm not going to a better place, unless that's what oblivion is, a few kilometres from here and the driver will pull over into a siding and ask would we like something to drink. He'll take out the big bottle of pre-mixed orange cordial and pour us each a cup. And like all the others the system couldn't handle— Polly, poor Polly! she tried—thus will end our relocation. They're killing us, all those who go and don't come back, all those who like the papers in the wheelie bin have become an extravagant waste. Polly, the Angel of Mercy, was all along the Angel of Death, with her clipboard marking up the fate of the condemned. I will not sit under the tree with my partner tomorrow in the early spring sun, watching the white cockatoos flap and roll—she will come back from her touring and find me gone, the table down, the bed unmade. He's been relocated, Büchner will say, and she—sweet innocence!—will smile, believing that finally my time has come: I'm out there getting paid, one day soon she'll see my name in the papers, they will have a photo of me, she'll ring me up, I'll hold her close, she'll retire, I'll pay all the bills, we'll move to our own house in a leafy suburb and I will write in my office at the end of the yard where rosellas will peck seed from the sill.

The bus is now crawling slowly around the gravel track towards the road. I look out the window: the party on the paddock is winding down, people with torches and candles are moving up the grassy bank, some are drifting back down the track towards the shed, others are jumping the boundary fence and walking towards the centre of the oval. Some people pass very close to the bus—can they see me inside? They look up at the window but their eyes look through me. Am I dead already? There are so many of them, *too many*—can Polly really expect to get on top of the problem with mathematics like this? A dozen of us, while hundreds are still trooping towards the trestle tables, asking to be fed. Asking to be fed. I look out the window, look behind—hundreds of them, like zombies. Then it hits me. I've not been condemned, I've been saved! *This* is the denouement. No-one can provide support to three hundred aspiring writers. They're walking to their deaths, we are driving to our freedom. Like zombies they walk in streams up the grassy bank, their faces ghostly, ready to sit down to their evening meal, never to get up again.

The bus turns, I strain my neck to see behind me but the oval, the camp, the people are gone. So *we* have been saved? I look back down the bus; everyone is very quiet. But stop, I want to say, so what if we are chosen, so what if we survive—how will we live with our consciences? Three hundred of our kind have been left behind—how will we live with that? I think these things but I cannot say them. I have half-raised myself in my seat. A few rows in front of me, just behind the driver, one of the passengers turns around. It's Judd. (When did he get on? I didn't see him get on.) He gives me a smile, then turns forward again. I'm on a bus with Polly-fuckers? I'm here because I've pleasured her, not because I can write? I look around at the other heads, men and women. Polly, her apple smell, the dark of her nipples, the cream of her thighs—is that all that binds us together? All the other aspiring writers, some good, some bad, some mediocre, sitting down to their poison pies— and we go free because we gave the whore what she wants?

The bus turns again, off the dirt road and onto the bitumen. I look out the window; under an almost-full moon the fences, the paddocks, the wheatfields look ghostly and strange. We drive and drive. The landscape doesn't change. Now the monitor above the driver's head flickers on and starts scrolling a piracy warning. Judd gets up from his seat—he's holding a big square Tupperware container. He starts walking down the aisle, distributing sandwiches wrapped in grease-proof paper to each of the passengers. When he hands me my sandwich he gives me what I can't help thinking is a warm and genuine smile. The video starts—it's *Chinatown*, with Jack Nicholson; we fade in on a black and white photograph, a man and a woman. A voice groans. I unwrap my sandwich but I don't feel hungry. The man looking at the photo throws something at the wall. Judd puts the Tupperware container in an overhead locker and sits back down in his seat. A new story is unfolding, H—— is far behind me now, I've already let it go. You've got to move on. Perhaps we're not all Polly-fuckers, perhaps Judd is here for the sandwiches, the paperwork at the other end? Perhaps I am here because of my Laburnum story, because my Laburnum story is good? Now the other character in the scene with Jack Nicholson is sobbing, tearing at the blinds. I look out the window. Still the same. I half-close my eyes. I open them again. Jack Nicholson pours a shot of bourbon. I watch for a little while longer then close my eyes again.

two

The bus stops. It's morning. I must have slept for hours. We're in a country town somewhere. I can see wide streets with footpaths and houses. A big country town. The driver gets out of the bus. Some passengers are still asleep, some are just waking up now. I raise myself in my seat a little and look out through the windscreen. The driver is standing in front of a high wire mesh gate, sorting through his keys. Now I see where we are—it's a school, a secondary school, but it's been closed down; all around as far as I can see is a high wire mesh fence topped with strands of barbed wire. The grounds are overgrown with weeds; leaf litter and bits of rubbish are piled up in corners where the wind has blown them. The building is one of those long drab 1970s types, clad with pressed-pebble-and-concrete slabs. The gum trees planted as saplings when the school was built have now grown into giants, dropping gumnuts, bark and whole branches onto the asphalt.

The driver finds the key he's been looking for and opens the padlock on the gate. He swings it back, first one side, then the other, and climbs back into the bus. He takes a moment at the top of the step to look around at his passengers—everyone looks expectantly back at him. But he doesn't say anything, he sits back down in his seat, puts the bus in gear and drives up to the front steps of the school. He stops again, the brakes hiss; he turns off the ignition. You can stretch your legs now if you want, he says, but don't wander too far. He steps down out of the bus again and through the side window I can see him wandering away a little, lighting a cigarette, then standing there on the asphalt, smoking.

The passengers begin to stir, tentatively at first: standing up, stretching, looking at their watches. They must have multiplied during the night. Is it just me, I think, or are there more now than when we started? I do a quick head count: twenty-three. I count again. Yes, there are more, but curiously Judd the factotum is no longer with us. We must have picked up some people in the night, and when we did, Judd must have left us. For good? I check all the heads again. Some passengers are now taking the driver at his word, walking down the aisle to the steps. Men, women, young, old—it's all as much a mystery as before. The new passengers, the ones who must have got on in the night, are also carrying folders, but theirs are blue plastic, the envelope type, with the little velcro tab to keep them closed. I watch as the passengers, in ones and twos, stand up and make their way down the aisle, some brushing past me from behind and smiling down at me as they pass.

I'm one of the last to get out of the bus: it's cool outside, it's rained overnight, and there's a heavy metallic smell coming off the wet asphalt. I can also smell the rich aroma of wet gum leaves, of rotting humus, damp earth, and a faint whiff of diesoline. I go and sit on the front steps of the school; I put my folder in my lap and start jiggling my knees. We're obviously waiting for someone or something—the driver has finished his cigarette and butted it out with his shoe and is now sitting on a bench seat under a nearby tree and he too is jiggling his knees. The bus makes a kind of ticking sound. How far did we travel? Were we driving all night? A woman walks over to the driver and asks him a question: he points behind him and the woman goes in that direction. She must have asked him about the toilets. A middle-aged man is walking about, swinging his arms back and forth, stretching his neck from side to side. He's getting ready to get back on the bus, I think, limbering up for the next part of the journey. So is this only a stopover, a rest break? But just as I am thinking this, a car arrives and pulls up beside the bus. It's an early model white Laser hatchback, with a small dint in the front passenger side panel. A young man gets out— late twenties, early thirties—and walks past me up the front steps with a bunch of keys in his hand. The driver gets up from his seat. The young man opens the front door then walks back down the steps. I stand up. Everyone has stopped what they were doing, waiting for instructions. The young man leans over into the front seat of his car and takes out a briefcase which he then rifles through until he finds what he is looking for. He puts a piece of paper on the bonnet and the driver, knowing the routine, takes a pen and signs it. The young man glances through it, puts it back in his briefcase, then goes around to the back of his car and opens the boot. The bus starts up but a dozen or so people now start running back to it, calling out to the driver that they've left their folders on board. The rest of us stand and watch. The young man asks the person nearest to him to grab a box from the boot—he grabs the other, tucks it under his arm, closes the boot with his elbow and walks back up the steps. The people who'd panicked start filing back out of the bus with their folders; the reversing lights and the beeper come on, the bus backs out, points itself in the direction it originally came from and drives away. The young man calls out to us—This way now, please! Everyone moves up the steps. Someone holds the front door open and we all file through.

It's very cold inside the building, a cold concrete chill that gets right inside your bones. We gather in the open office area: the young man keeps stepping backwards until he is standing hard up against a door with a sign on it that says 'Principal'. Welcome, he says—could you please close the door? My name is Dean, we will soon be moving down to your classroom. The nearest toilets are in the breezeway at the end of the main corridor: boys to the right, girls to the left. The sick bay is just around the corner here to my left; the canteen is outside off the main corridor to the right. This area would normally be out of bounds. I will show you to your sleeping quarters later. All right then, off we go. After this brief and slightly pointless introduction he pushes his way back through the crowd, gesturing for his carrier to follow, and starts walking down what he called the main corridor until we come to an intersection with further corridors off to our left and right. Toilets down that way! he says. Canteen to the right! He turns left and we all follow. At the end of this corridor we turn right, climb a few steps and stop in front of an empty classroom. Outside, the schoolyard is deserted, leaves and bark are scattered across the asphalt, here and there a window has been smashed and there's graffiti on the walls. But aside from the dank smell and the thin layer of dust on the window ledges and lockers, the inside of the building is surprisingly intact.

The teacher—the young man (but no, he is obviously now 'the teacher')—takes out his keys and opens the classroom door. He drops his box on the front table—his carrier does the same—and puts his briefcase on the floor beside it. He waves us in. We file inside. It's actually very beautiful in here, in this room, the long walk has taken us from the southern to the north-eastern side of the building and the morning sun is streaming in through the wall of windows along one side. It's warmer than the office area by at least ten or more degrees. Through the windows I can see a basketball court and a grass playing area with a cluster of bench seats arranged under a big gum tree with dark sappy bark. Beyond that I can see the back fences and roofs of the adjoining houses. It's the strangest feeling, then, to think that just over there whole families are living normal lives. I can see clothes on a washing line, the top of a children's swing. Far away, way over there past the roof tops, I can see what looks like a TV or telephone tower. The overnight showers have cleared and the sky has broken blue.

People have started to take their seats at the tables arranged around the room, two chairs per table. I get one of the last window seats, right up the back of the classroom. There are names and love messages written on the desk; on the window ledge beside me are the papery bodies of dead blowflies. Someone takes the seat next to mine, a gawky man with square-framed glasses, while at the front of the class the teacher cleans algebraic calculations from the whiteboard with the end of his sleeve. Someone at the table in front opens their folder and starts arranging their papers. Very soon this action becomes infectious: without any specific instructions from the teacher everyone starts opening their folders and arranging their papers on their desks. The teacher meanwhile has opened the larger of the two boxes and taken out a TV monitor and a VCR. He sets them up on the front table with the monitor facing the class. All right, he says, beaming: holiday's over! With a black whiteboard marker he draws a straight line across the width of the whiteboard, quickly divides it into three sections by intersecting the horizontal line with two short vertical strokes (the middle section becoming the longest), then above the line he writes, in Roman numerals: I, II and III.

A holiday? A *holiday*. So that's all it was? The caravan, the tents, the long stretched-out days of summer. It was a holiday. We left the city, went to the country, found a campsite, made new friends, broke with old routines, renewed ourselves. The writer's life—it's a holiday! I wake up late, masturbate, linger over breakfast. Maybe if I'm lucky I write a dozen lines. At three o'clock a tidal wave of tiredness comes over me and I fall back into bed. I wake up an hour later, look out the caravan window, talk to myself about doing more work but of course I never do. I'm on holidays. I'm hanging the washing on the chrome rail at the front of my caravan, I'm shaking the sand from my shoes, I'm walking to the shower block with a towel slung over my shoulder and a sticky cake of soap in my hand. In the neighbouring caravans I can hear the other holiday-makers laughing, or arguing, or whispering quietly; out on the playground I can hear the dull pop of a tennis ball being hit. As evening falls the smell of barbecued meat drifts across the camp and outside their caravans and tents the adults sit and drink and talk while the children play their last game of hide-and-seek in the dark. I've been on holidays, that's what it was, and now I'm here to work.

These thoughts have both disturbed and enlivened me *(A holiday, all a holiday, and this now the real beginning?)* and I watch the teacher working at the whiteboard and see what he's doing with a very clear, very vivid eye. I look around me, the classroom, the students. Back to school, I think. Everyone is sitting up, straight-backed, looking at the whiteboard. The teacher has now written above his horizontal line the three words: SET-UP, CONFRONTATION, RESOLUTION. He steps back from the whiteboard and points to it with his marker. The Paradigm, he says. This word, 'paradigm', rings in the classroom air like a bell: shiny, silver, singingly clear. He walks back to the whiteboard and writes PARADIGM on it, in big capital letters. All right, he says, now let's put this paradigm to the test.

It's all moving too fast for me, I already feel like a dunce, like I've already fallen through the cracks. He's talking about *Chinatown*, of course, the movie on the bus, this is what he means by the paradigm and the test. But all I saw was the SET-UP, and even this small part I watched with my thoughts elsewhere. Soon I wasn't even watching at all but was looking through my reflection in the dark window out onto the moonlit fields and the fenceposts flashing past. Where are we going? Where are we off to now? Are we really the chosen few, off to something new, something better? And where is she now, my partner, she and her friends? Has she too found a better life? (We drifted apart, I don't know why—did I too quickly base everything on the elasticity of her flesh? We drifted apart and I fucked Polly and entered into this obscene agreement. But she now, where is she?) With these thoughts, the dark night, the moonlit landscape, the rhythm of the road, my eyelids began to droop and close. I didn't watch *Chinatown*, I didn't know I was supposed to (again—how many times?—I have confused recreation with work). Not long after Faye Dunaway made her first appearance in Jack Nicholson's office I was far away and sound asleep.

Now the teacher is asking questions and down the front especially people are throwing up their hands. The teacher points to the raised hands with his marker, dashing back and forth to the whiteboard and scribbling things on it. He's talking about structure, story structure, we're learning how to structure our work. The holiday's over. People are responding enthusiastically, throwing up their hands, calling out suggestions—Confrontation! says someone. Obstacles! says another. A story in pictures! says a third—and the teacher, like a prowling caged animal, lurches back and forth between these shouted suggestions and his increasingly frenetic-looking whiteboard. I have taken my Laburnum papers out of my folder and among them I have found some blank sheets; I put one of these sheets in front of me and at the top of this sheet I write the word PARADIGM and draw a line underneath it. Beneath that I draw a copy of the teacher's diagram with the marks and numbers on it and beneath that I start to write the words that out of the jumble on the whiteboard I think might be important. But very soon there are just too many words being shouted out and written down by the teacher. I start doodling: first I draw a face, then a stick figure body on it, then a whole lot of other stick-figure bodies, then all of them running over a cliff. Then for a while I just draw lines up and down along the border of my page: a bold line, then a thin line, then a bold line again, and then fancy swirls in the corner. The teacher has turned on the TV and the VCR; the piracy warning scrolls; he goes back to the whiteboard and reduces the amount of scribble on it until all that's left is the divided line and a few words and phrases written at all different angles around it. He circles the words 'a story in pictures' just as *Chinatown* starts and we fade in again on the full-screen photograph, the man and the woman making love, then Jack Nicholson under the fan and the other character down the wall.

While I concentrate very hard this time on the movie I realise that the gawky man with the glasses sitting next to me has meanwhile slipped a folded piece of paper across the table so that it is sticking out a little from under the sheet of paper I have been doodling on. His eyes are looking towards the front of the class, ostensibly watching the movie too, but around his mouth I can see the unmistakable signs of a smile. I unfold the piece of paper, keeping my eyes to the front, then quickly glance down at it. *Fuck the paradigm*, it says. I smile, and fold the paper up again. Suddenly everything in the classroom goes quiet. The video has been paused—the frozen image of Jack Nicholson leaning back in his chair quivers slightly—and the teacher is standing beside it with his hands on his hips. Are we all right? he says. Are we all right up the back there? You, he says, pointing to my neighbour: what main elements of the story set-up have we seen so far? My neighbour doesn't answer, but he can't wipe the smile from his face. You might think it's all a big joke now, mister, says the teacher, his hands still firmly planted on his hips, but come exam time we might wipe that smile from your face. There's a very heavy silence in the room now—everyone knew they had to take all this very seriously but no-one, not even the teacher's pets down the front, thought it might get as serious as *this*. Exams? Even my neighbour, who in his short time in the spotlight had happily assumed the role of class clown, is no longer smiling. It might just be worth reiterating, the teacher is saying, before we go any further, that each and every one of you is very lucky to be here. Your former colleagues—let's just say they have fallen by the wayside. You can hold on to your romantic dreams all you like, I'm sure some of you still do, but the fact is there is only one way to make a living out of telling stories and that is by having your stories told on celluloid within the paradigm of a three-act structure—something that, I remind you, you lucky people now have the opportunity of doing, should you choose to take it. I don't want to play 'the teacher', he says, I'm just here to help you get out of the writing rut you were in, but if any of you are not prepared to listen and learn, then please, there's the door. The teacher has taken his left hand off his hip and is pointing at the door with the index finger of it. There is a substantial pause. Right, he says, satisfied: then let's get back to work!

We watch *Chinatown* all morning, the teacher sometimes pushing the pause button and pointing out a story feature to us. I take notes, so does my neighbour—so, as far as I can see, do the rest of the class—and we make no more contact with each other until the bell goes for morning recess. Then, as the teacher rewinds the tape and people start putting down their pens I see my neighbour tearing off the bottom corner of the piece of paper he has been writing on. He pushes it across towards me. The writing is minuscule, spidery thin. *The axe for the frozen sea*, it says. He stands up, still not looking at me, and makes his way to the door. I push the tiny piece of paper into my folder, close it, and stand up too.

Out in the playground, the first thing I notice is how incredibly hungry I am. I've had no breakfast, I've not eaten since yesterday at lunch. People are standing around, alone or in little groups, but I can't see my neighbour anywhere. I make my way over to a group with a drift of blue-grey smoke above it and ask one of them can I borrow a cigarette? I have not smoked for months, have strangely felt no desire to do so (perhaps if I'd gone with the actors I would?) but the first drag on this begged cigarette is a wonderful thing. I'm starving, and the rush of nicotine both stills the gnawing in my belly and makes me feel all light in the head. I move away from the group—I feel, not antisocial, just a bit tired and confused—and find a sunny spot by the wall of the building. I put my back against the pebble slab and feel its warmth seep into me. I drag on my cigarette, blowing the smoke upward, watching the play of light as it drifts away from me. So this is it, I think, I'm back at school, I'm going to do my lessons all over again. This time, they tell me, it won't be wasted; I won't end up spending long uneventful days in cheap falling-down houses, butting my cigarettes out on the concrete, watching the blossom buds form on the plum tree, the planes flying in overhead; I won't go off in my caravan and toast marshmallows on a fork; I will learn everything I have to learn, to do better, to get on. This is my chance,

I think, it's all been put on a plate for me: I'm special, I'm one of the privileged few. If I listen carefully, try harder, put an end to this wasteful cynicism, this facetiousness, this irony, if I can just get *serious* for a change (it's only seriousness that gets taken seriously), put my head down, stop fucking around, then perhaps now, soon, finally, things might start working for me.

The bell rings; recess is over. People start filing back into class. I butt my cigarette out on the wall behind me, twisting and turning it into the small concrete hollow where one of the pebbles has fallen out. Back in the class-room the seat beside me is empty—my neighbour, the gawky man with the glasses, has been moved to the front of the class. He sits on his own at a table directly in front of the teacher's, who is just now opening the flaps of the second box. From it he takes a pile of shrink-wrapped packets of 8 x 10 white filing cards and starts placing a packet each in front of us on our desks. We are to use them, he is saying, to identify the principal units of action in our story. Let's write these units of action down in note form on our cards, he says, then place them in order on our desks and see what sort of 'story pattern' emerges. For the next two hours until lunchtime I sit at my desk and shuffle my cards, looking out the window, looking up at the whiteboard, looking at the teacher, who too many times then looks up at me. After about half an hour I write on the filing card on the top of my pile the words *Horse and dray arrives in clearing* and then some time in the following hour *Ernest Fairweather is chopping a tree.* Then about half an hour before the lunch bell rings the teacher tells us all to stop what we are doing. He points to a woman near the front of the class and asks her to read aloud from her cards. As she reads them out one by one— she's got fifteen, I've got two—the teacher recreates them diagrammatically on the whiteboard by drawing rough rectangles, writing what the woman says in them and then connecting each 'card' with a short line from it to its immediate neighbour. It's like a flow chart. Above this flow chart the teacher writes, again in big capital letters: DRAMATIC STRUCTURE. Many people quickly write this down. I look at the rectangles and from what I can make of the woman's story it is one of a young girl from the wrong side of the tracks who stumbles helplessly through a world of drugs, crime, prostitution and damaged relationships until her final, if ambiguous, redemption. The teacher is now dashing back and forth around the whiteboard, pointing here, pointing there. He'll suddenly rub out the contents of one rectangle, transfer the contents of another into it and then the contents of the original into the one he's just emptied. He's rearranging the pieces. He underlines the word STRUCTURE at the top of the white-board and now, taking suggestions openly from the class, continues to move the contents of his rectangles around.

It should be interesting, I know it should, it should have me on the edge of my seat. It's the new beginning, it's why I'm here, but I can barely keep my eyes open; my mind keeps drifting, my eyes keep drooping; I keep thinking about dim sims, it's absurd, but I can't help it; I see in my mind's eye a bright-lit bain-marie with soft steam rising from the edges of the steel tray. There are pies in it, potato cakes, some chips, but as in my mind's eye I stand there looking in through the steam-shrouded glass, what my mind's eye is drawn to inexorably are the two fried dim sims sitting in a compartment on their own. I point to them with my finger and can feel the heat coming off the glass. The lady picks them up one by one with her tongs and places them in a small brown paper bag. She asks do I want sauce, the bottle already in her hand, and then at my signal puts the nozzle inside the bag and shakes it a few times up and down. She hands me the bag, I hand her the money; as she steps sideways to the register to ring up the transaction and get my change I bring the bag up a little towards my nose. The bell rings. It's lunchtime. I can taste the cold saliva sliding down the insides of my cheeks. People are packing up their folders, the teacher is speaking—I hear the word 'canteen' and then very little after that; my stomach literally heaves involuntarily inside me, stirred to an uncontrollable pitch of excitement by the sudden conjunction of my food fantasy and the many possibilities the word 'canteen' has stirred in my imagination. The rest of the class too, though retaining their decorum, have responded spontaneously to this word 'canteen'. They are all up, mentally recalling the teacher's earlier directions to it. As his concluding words trail off behind them many are already pushing their way to the door.

I end up near the end of the canteen queue, which means I have some time to piece together with my own mental filing cards a story to go with the picture I now see before me. There are probably about eighteen people in front of me, corralled between the two steel-pipe rails, worn smooth over the years by thousands of young hands. The person at the front of the queue walks away with a small brown paper bag in their hand. It is then, just before the queue shuffles forwards again, that I am able to get a glimpse of Judd, behind the counter, serving the food. *(Judd, I think, Polly's lapdog?)* I step forward, moving the filing cards around in my head. So he left the bus, I think, he must have, sometime in the night, probably when I was asleep, probably at some far-off country petrol station where he picked up the waiting station wagon. (I see it very clearly, this station wagon, this is what the teacher meant by visualising: a late-model green Subaru Outback with two T's in the registration number.) Then, following a brief sleep in the front seat, he drove this green Subaru to the big town nearby where at the twenty-four-hour super-market he bought (with the petty cash Polly had given him), from the frozen foods section, two or three jumbo-sized packs of dim sims. He then loaded this shopping into the station wagon and drove out to the school. He gave the canteen a quick spring clean (presumably while we were having our morning lessons) then stocked the fridge and plugged the fryer in.

I reach the front of the queue: Judd looks up at me, then looks away again. It's sausage rolls, he says. I keep looking at him. *(Sausage rolls?)* He blurts a bit of tomato sauce into a small brown paper bag and hands it out to me. I grip the edge but suddenly he is leaning over very close to my face, a handsome young man with piercing blue eyes. The actors are coming tonight, he whispers, to workshop your scenes tomorrow. Listen, it's not right, but I might be able to get you some time with your partner. He looks me in the eye, holds eye contact for a moment—a disturbing, frightened look—then releases his grip on the bag.

I make my way across the playground, the brown paper bag in my hand. *She is coming? Here?* But how will

I look her in the eye? She with her wild and spontaneous ways, her work structured to no paradigm; free, fluid, formless; immersed utterly in the present tense, the now? How will I explain to her the diagram on the blackboard, the school bell each day dividing those days into three, me going over all my old lessons again? I've now reached the tree on the far side of the playground with a bench seat beneath it. There's a big brick building behind me. I sit on my own—most of the others are gathered near the canteen, standing in groups, sitting on the seats, some sitting cross-legged on the asphalt in the sun. But the most unsettling thing of all, I think, as I bite into my sausage roll, is the fact that, if Judd is just a lowly canteen hand, as he certainly appears to be, then he's clearly been given no special privileges for his pleasuring of Polly—and, if that is the case, I think, pursuing things logically, then perhaps nor have I? I bite the sausage roll again. Perhaps I was not put on that last bus for the pleasure (or otherwise) I had given her, perhaps I was not chosen for my cunt-licking but for my *talent and integrity*? Perhaps, just perhaps, my Laburnum story is *good*. Of all the trash that was produced back there and which for the most part ended up in the big blue wheelie bin, perhaps my work *had something in it*? And if I were to apply myself to my lessons, I think, use the paradigm and listen carefully to what my teacher says, well, very possibly—*it is possible*—I might create work worthy of the support given to me. I bite again into the sausage roll and chew it, going over this last thought. A story, I think, a real story, with a beginning, middle and end...?

I spend the rest of lunchtime like this: contemplating the meaning of Judd's appearance, eating my sausage roll, letting my eye rove over my fellow students in the playground. Someone has found an old tennis ball and two people are playing a game of handball up against the canteen wall. I still can't see my gawky neighbour and when we go back into class after lunch I see that his seat—his new seat, the one in front of the teacher—is empty. The teacher has meanwhile cleaned the whiteboard and begun to write a new lesson up on it. Everyone starts taking their seats—there's a low murmur of conversation, a shuffling of papers—and I can see the teacher glancing over his shoulder, mentally ticking off the numbers as they dribble back into class. On the whiteboard, in capital letters, he has written the words SET-UP and beneath it a diagram of a starter shooting his pistol. He steps back from the whiteboard, does a quick silent head count, then crosses to the door and slides it shut. He points back across the room to the whiteboard—all the students look at it—then from his position at the door he points the remote control at the VCR. He's skipped the piracy warning this time; we come straight in on the black and white photograph and the groan. The first ten pages, says the teacher loudly, crossing back to his desk: the first ten pages, that's all you've got—let's look now at our first ten pages.

Dense scrub. Hammering rain. The shapes of bushes spectral in the moonlight. In the distance we see the light of a lamp approaching, moving in and out between the trees. As the light approaches, we see its source in clearer detail. It's a Tilley lamp, held high by one of two figures on the seat of a dray. We see the dark shapes of the figures, one with a wide-brimmed hat, one wearing a blanket like a cowl, and the broad back and flanks of the horse. The driver pulls on the reins. The dray halts. The lamp rocks backwards and forwards, revealing in flashes a scrubby clearing. The figure in the hat ties off the reins and gets down from the dray. The other figure stands up, and holds the lamp high above her head. We see her face: young, dark, mysterious, beautiful.

I work like this all afternoon, I have never tried so hard in all my life. I cross out one beginning and start another, then another one after that. I pull my sentences apart into such small pieces that they are hardly sentences at all any more, they are like kindergarten building blocks, with letters and pictures of animals on them. I put up my hand and call the teacher over and suffer his breath as he leans over and helps me more clearly identify my underlying dramatic premise. I am writing a film, I am doing what I'm told, I am pouring my story into my structure. I've convinced myself—I've had to—that my Laburnum story is good (that's why I'm here) and that with proper management it can become the product the teacher reassures me it will. I just have to learn my lessons—I've never listened to my lessons, that was my trouble, they were around me everywhere, chattering away, but I never listened to them. And when she arrives—today? tomorrow?—and sees me in my grey shorts, white knee-length socks and black patent leather shoes, my short back and sides, my pimple-face, and thinks me childish, a dunce, and says with a bitter-sweet voice: Look at you, you still haven't learned your lessons—I will show her my set-up, my heroic characters, vividly sketched, the dark rain-swept clearing, the first story clues, and everything will change. I cannot think about the hundreds back at H——: the pies, the vomiting, the shuddering limbs, the bodies piled into ute trays, the farmer's tractor digging a hole way out over there where no-one will see. I cannot think about my gawky neighbour, gone. It is a ruthless business, this is the chief lesson I have had to learn: do not listen to your inner voice, do not strike out on paths untrod, do not believe in higher things, don't make your sentences too long—look at the paradigm, listen to your teachers, learn your lessons. Don't waste sympathy on those not chosen. They are already in the ditch, the tractor is already covering them over, soon they'll be sown with seeds and a herd of cows will graze on their memory. Farmer, butcher, chef: vomiting, shuddering, all in the hole. You can't help it if you're special, if you've been picked out like this—it's not because of what you did with Polly, that much is clear—look at Judd, where did it get him? It's because you have something to work with and because you're prepared to *learn*. This is what no-one, with the exception of the hand-picked members of this class, was actually prepared to do. They were all on holidays, and they thought this holiday would last forever.

The man reaches up with his hand and helps the woman step down from the dray. While the woman holds the lamp high above her head, the man takes a tent from under the seat and heaves it onto his shoulder. The horse snorts and bucks its head. In the

circle of yellow lamplight we watch the man kick some
fallen branches aside and throw the tent roll to the
ground.

It is very pleasant at my desk, the sun streaming in through the windows from outside, the classroom quiet, each student bent over their work. The teacher moves among us, sometimes stopping to give advice in a soft, soothing tone of voice. I watch the shadows changing, in the playground, on the windowsill beside me; the afternoon drifts by. It is almost home-time when I look out the window and see the Transit van pulling up outside. The driver's door opens and Andrew gets out. He looks shorter than before. There's someone sitting in the passenger seat but I can't tell yet if it's her—at this distance, with the sun on the other side of the car, all I can make out is a dark human shape. I glance back inside the classroom, some of the other students have seen the Transit van and are looking out the window too. The teacher still has his head down, he is leaning over a desk near the front of the class, looking carefully at a student's work. I look out the window again. Now I can see Judd approaching quickly across the playground. He takes exceptionally long strides, he almost looks like Groucho Marx. More students are looking out the window; the teacher looks up too. Excuse me? he says, in a patronising tone. Everyone hunches back over their work. From under my eyebrows, though, my head lowered just enough for my eyes not to be seen, I watch the teacher move over to the window and study for a while the goings-on outside. By a slight, very subtle rotation of my head and by pushing my pupils as far across to the left in their sockets as they will go, I am then able to see Judd arriving at the Transit van. Andrew is leaning on the bonnet, waiting for him. Judd gestures, first to somewhere behind him, indicating, I imagine, the place where Andrew was supposed to park, then towards the classroom, indicating why it was best they didn't park there. Andrew looks directly towards us; with my face almost in my folder I watch him out of the corner of my eye. Does he see me? Is that toss of the head him laughing at the very idea? Her former boyfriend, back at school, trying to get some qualifications! Judd finishes his instructions and begins striding back the way he came. The passenger door opens—it's her, she gets out, asks a question; Andrew points, first towards Judd, then towards the classroom. She looks in my direction; yes, she's looking at me. I hold my gaze, I feel all faint, across this unbridgeable distance I feel the most intense love go out. I'm just a schoolboy, and she with her hair and her curves is my unattainable fantasy. Andrew gets back into his side of the

Transit van, she gets back into hers. Like a couple, I think. She's telling the kids in the back to be quiet. Her husband doesn't love her, not in the way she could be loved: here, over here in this classroom, this schoolboy here, he's the one to give you a love both pure and rare.

The Transit van starts up and moves back across the playground. All finished now? the teacher asks. He's looking down across a row of heads at me. Without realising it, I have been subtly moving my head in the direction of the Transit van and it is this small but telling movement that the teacher has seen. I look up at him. Back to work, he says. I lower my head again but not without one quick glance out at the now-deserted playground. So Judd was not lying, I think, she really has come. Tomorrow I will see her, if not tonight. Will we still know each other? Can we pick up from where we left off?

It is three o'clock when the teacher calls pens down. I've done almost nothing. Tomorrow we will be focusing principally on our characters, says the teacher. He calls for our work—Hand it down, he says—and each student hands what they have written to the table in front of them, and so on, until the work forms little piles on the tables at the very front of the class. The teacher collects them up. He will select one or two for workshopping tomorrow, he says, when we will then have some actors to help bring our characters to life: some of you may have already seen them arriving. He's looking at me, and he's smiling. With my back up straight and both hands flat on the desk I smile back at him. No, I'm not the teacher's pet, but I don't think I'm the troublemaker either. The teacher puts the big pile of papers on his desk. He looks at his watch—and just then the end-of-school bell rings.

three

Judd appears in the doorway, throwing a basketball back
and forth from one hand to the other. We're going to go
out and play for a while, to 'blow away the cobwebs', the
teacher says. Down the corridor and out the door at the
end into the playground, my eye keeps scouting everywhere for her. Perhaps they've gone? Perhaps Judd was
sending them away? I will die if I don't see her soon, I
think—it is not desire, I don't even know any more what
desire means, I just want to talk, ask her again what she
makes of all this, see if she is as confused and beaten by it
all as me. No, I think, as we cross the playground to the
basketball court: no, be careful, that's not what you want
to say, that's not what you want to say at all. You want first
to take an interest in *her* work, all the things she's seen
and done, you want to listen carefully, patiently, before

telling her with no great fanfare about yourself. How you got selected because your Laburnum story was good, how you've proved yourself willing to learn; you'll tell her about the paradigm and the importance of structure and all the other things you've been taught.

I want to keep going on with these thoughts, would happily keep rehearsing them in my head all afternoon, but now we are at the basketball court and Judd is dividing us up into teams. No-one wants to do this, it is obvious from the body language, but no-one knows how to say no to him either. We've been up half the night, we've only had one meal, all we want now is to rest, to sleep. Even the brave faces on the teacher's pets are caving in: we're dog-tired, we're hungry; give us a meal and put us to bed— tomorrow we'll be better off for it. But where are we going to sleep? I look at the players lining up opposite me: they don't know either. Are they going to put us to sleep here in the school, somewhere in town—are we special enough to warrant hotel rooms of our own? Or are we going to get back on the bus and travel all night again to—where? No. I'm trotting back down the court now, to take up my position in defence. Surely I've not got it all wrong? That we are out on 'day leave' only? That we're only filling in time now till the bus arrives, perhaps a real school bus that must first drop off its real school children? And that then we'll be put on it and taken back to H——, just in time for dinner, and then wake up tomorrow and do it again? And what will we go back to if we do? Will it be a ghost camp? Or already filled with new arrivals? Will Polly still be there, her red slash of a mouth, her frightened eyes? Judd has blown the whistle, someone grabs the ball from the air and throws it in my direction. Someone in front of me catches it and throws it back. It's a farce. No-one has the energy to take it seriously. I'm sure I'm not the only one thinking about the sleeping arrangements. The ball goes back and forth like this for some time—you'd swear the two teams were throwing it to each other—until suddenly, out of nowhere, someone flings the ball towards the ring at the opposite end and scores a goal. A muted cheer goes up. Judd retrieves the ball and runs back to the centre of the court with it.

It is almost by accident that I then look back at the classroom and see the figures moving around inside. I can see the teacher, near the window, pointing, and moving past him as a dark shadow two figures carrying a table. It's the actors. They're pushing back the furniture to make a performance space for tomorrow: we'll sit in our chairs and watch them bring our characters to life. Then from these dark shapes one in particular seems to step out of the shadows towards me. It's her. She puts down her end of the table and stands next to the teacher, talking to him. He points variously around the room then turns and points out the window. She turns too. The low-down late afternoon sun lights her up, all straws and magentas, her hair ablaze. She looks out towards me. I look at her. Then I crash to the ground. Someone has thrown the basketball at my head. I was supposed to catch it. You were supposed to catch it, says Judd, standing above me.

I'm taken to the sick bay and left there with a minder, a middle-aged man with a goatee beard and silver-framed glasses. Judd says I can stay there till dinner. Dinner, I think. It takes a while to staunch the bleeding. I lie on the narrow bed—it smells musty, and very faintly of stale urine—with a twisted tissue up each nostril and a damp dishcloth on my forehead. My minder sits on the chair beside me. You should have been watching, he says. I let it go. Then after a very long pause, I say: I saw my partner, at the window. There's an equally long pause. Do you think we will sleep here tonight? I ask. He thinks I mean here in the sick bay, he and I, together. I don't mean here, I say, I mean somewhere in the school? He shrugs. He seems to think I am beneath him. I wonder, I say—half to my minder, half to myself—if we are any more special than the others, the ones we left behind? He doesn't answer. You know, I say, I saw Polly yesterday afternoon *(Yesterday?*

Was that yesterday?) going around the camp; maybe she'd just drawn all those names out of a hat? My minder looks at me—it's not a pleasant look. This is the last place he wants to be—he could be out there, making an impression *(On whom? The factotum, Judd?)* but instead he's in here, looking after the klutz. I study the side of his face for a while: You'll go far, I think.

We don't speak again. It must be an hour or more spent like that, turning the dishcloth over, dabbing each nostril with a tissue, my minder staring intently at the door, before Judd comes back to get us. He opens the door, asks how I am feeling, and says we'll be eating soon. My minder leaves first, anxious to put this humiliation behind him, then, just as I get to the door, the damp dishcloth still around my neck, Judd suddenly turns and pushes me back inside. He has a look almost of horror on his face. I shouldn't be doing this, he says. He thrusts a tightly folded piece of paper into my hand. I unfold the note. It's in her handwriting. *Meet me in the gym at eight*, it says.

With my bruised face and this message in my head it's hard to concentrate on or really engage with anything that follows. I watch it all from far away, counting down the minutes, wondering what I will say to her, what she will say to me. I leave the sick bay with the note folded up in my pocket and follow Judd and the minder down the corridor. It's getting dark outside, it must be about six o'clock now, or later—we've in fact been in the sick bay for hours—and a gloaming light falls through the windows on either side of the main corridor. We're heading back towards the classroom; we turn left at the main intersection; Judd and the minder are talking now, I can hear snatches of what they're saying—it's about story, structure, the set-up, what we learned today and what we will do tomorrow—and as we approach the next intersection and the stairs I can see the light from a room spilling into the corridor. At the top of the stairs all the class are gathered: this is a few doors down from our classroom; they have obviously been told to wait there for Judd's return. They all step back. The minder joins the group and blends immediately into it; I stand a little off to one side. Judd takes up a position in front of the nearest classroom door and, playing with a bunch of keys, addresses us directly. Okay, he says, there are three rooms for sleeping: 212, 213 and 214. This is 213. He takes a key and opens the door, sliding it back with one hand while reaching for the light switch with the other. The fluorescent lights inside flicker on. We all push forward towards the doorway and the head-high windows along the corridor. There are no tables and chairs inside; all across the floor in an interlocking pattern are about a dozen single mattresses with sleeping bags or blankets on them. Judd gives us time to take in this scene then he flicks the light off in that room and opens the door of the one opposite. We won't bother about who sleeps where, he says, smiling: I'll let you sort that out later. He flicks the light on. The same again. It's the same in 214. This is where Dean and I will sleep, he says, pointing into that room, and tonight our guests will be in here too. Our guests, I think: *where are our guests?* We move down the corridor. The next room is locked and dark, inside are all the tables and chairs from the other rooms, stacked almost to the ceiling. We pass our class-room; it too is locked. All right then, says Judd, let's eat!

We reach the last room in the corridor, the biggest of them all in this wing. All the lights are on inside. There are tables arranged in two long rows with chairs on either side. The actors have already sat down to their meals: I see her, three places down from the far end of the table near the window. She has her back to me. She's not sitting next to Andrew, he's sitting on the other side a few seats down from her and now, as I enter the room along with the other writers, he looks up, sees me and smiles. I smile awkwardly back. I know she will turn around any minute, I'm trying to look but not look; I see Andrew lean down the table towards her, obviously telling her I am here, but just at that moment Judd is calling our attention to the two big tables of food parked under the classroom whiteboard and I am forced to turn my back. I look at the whiteboard and the writing on it. *Please form a queue and help yourself*, it says. There is an arrow pointing down to the food. I join the queue, and look back over towards her—but now she has her back turned to me again. The teacher enters: he's changed his clothes, had a shower, I can smell his after-shave even from where I am standing. He stops to chat to a couple of people in the queue then moves over to the tables. Andrew gets up, the teacher shakes his hand. She still won't turn around.

I take a plate and choose from the things laid out on the table: pastas mostly, and salads, and French sticks sliced and buttered. Did Judd make all this? I take my plate and sit down near the front of the table closest to the door—I don't know why but I can't go close, I can't go up and tell her: Here I am. I bend over and eat my meal. One sausage roll for lunch—I have never been so hungry in all my life. I keep glancing at her face in half-profile; I can just see her nose, her lips, her chin. Has she seen me, is she waiting for me to go over? Why should we be so distant? We who were once so close? There are jugs of water on the table—some plastic, some glass, all different—but no alcohol. So this is what it means to be professional? I pour myself a glass of water and take a sip. The teacher has joined the actors' table with his plate of food and he in turn is joined by the usual bunch of sycophants who lean towards him and laugh at his jokes. He's off-duty now—charming, ebullient—sharing his own stories of his student theatre days: There were plenty of actors around better than me!

I keep looking at the side of her face—I can see she's not laughing but is she smiling at least? She must be smiling. Can she afford not to? Judd is the last to fill his plate and now he sits down at my table on the opposite side a few places down—not directly in my line of sight but close enough for me to think it is deliberate. He smiles at the person next to him and shares a quick joke then starts on his meal. He's about to bring his fork to his mouth when he looks at me, straight at me and no-one else. But I simply cannot interpret his look. He holds it for a few seconds, his fork suspended halfway to his mouth; he's looking at me as if—no, he's just looking at me, he's just saying: Look, I'm looking at you. He's not saying: I'm *watching* you, be careful, or anything like that. He's just looking at me, that's all. He lifts his fork and breaks the look and gives himself over to his meal. I'm about to do the same, then I see her stand up. She pushes the chair back, says something to her neighbour, briefly has eye contact with the teacher, then walks down the aisle between the tables. She passes so close to me that I can feel the gentle breeze in her wake. She keeps her eyes resolutely on the door. She slides it open, steps out into the corridor, then slides it shut again.

Go. Should I go now? I look around the room. Those who looked up at her have gone back to their meals. There's nothing in it, I think, she's drunk too much water and has gone to the toilet. I gesture to the person a few places down the table to hand me the jug. I fill my glass and drink it down, slowly, evenly, with long steady draughts. I put my glass back down on the table. I look around the room. I'm just going to the toilet, I say, to the person opposite me. He looks up, wondering why I've bothered him with this news—but I'm already up and gone.

Out in the corridor I slide the door quietly shut behind me. I'm not sure which way she's gone. I bob down so I can't be seen through the high corridor windows and work my way like that to the end of the dinner room. There's enough light spilling out through these windows to light the stairs and I carefully pick my way down them, one hand on the rail. A piece of chewing gum has been stuck to it, no doubt years ago, and I feel the smooth hard ridge of it with my hand. At the bottom of the stairs I stop to get my bearings—but the trouble is I have no idea where the gymnasium is. The teacher made no mention of it, most likely so that people like me would not go stumbling around in the dark trying to find it. Besides, that was the message from Judd, to meet her in the gym, but why of all people should I trust him? Perhaps she *was* just going to the toilet and if I stood here long enough I would see her coming back; then I would stop her, say: Here, it's me—we would hug, kiss, and go back to our meals together. Why did I ever let us separate in the first place? But no, I think, this time I have to trust Judd. His look, the way she deliberately avoided looking at me, these are not figments of my imagination. I look around again. Behind me are the stairs leading back to our living quarters, to my right a short corridor with a door leading out to the playground, to my left the corridor that connects this to the main one, straight ahead of me the continuation of the one I am in: I can see a little way down it, a couple of doors, the lockers lining one wall, then it is all swallowed up by the dark. I'm about to venture in that direction—nothing ventured, nothing gained, I think—when I see a figure coming towards me from out of the corridor to my left. Is it her? Is that her? It's not. It's the actor I'd sat next to in the Transit van that day. Marti. Marti, I say. She stops, and looks strangely at me. She doesn't know who I am. I worked with you, once, I say. She smiles, but I know she's covering up. Wayne, I say. Then she remembers. But then, almost simultaneously, she is pricked by the memory. Her eyes glaze over. She knows me, but she doesn't want to know me, doesn't want anyone to know she knows me. Do you know where the gym is? I ask. She shrugs her shoulders. Maybe that way, she says. She points back to where she has just come from and lets the gesture hang in the air for a moment: she's thinking, she has something she wants to say, but then just as quickly she drops her arm and with it the unspoken thought. Anyway, she says, nice to see you again—and with that she's gone, back up the stairs towards the dinner room light.

I watch her go—what *did* she want to say?—then go back to my dilemma of which corridor to take. Though it seems ridiculous under the circumstances to take Marti's word for it I decide to go where she has pointed, back towards the main corridor. I start walking in that direction. It's dark where I am now, and eerily quiet. There is a three-quarter moon in the sky outside, sliding in and out as if on shifting plates between the clouds, and shreds of this moonlight fall through the corridor windows, dusting the floor with a strange luminescence. When the moon goes in behind the clouds I have to hold one hand out beside me and let my fingers bump along the rows of lockers for guidance; eventually, in this way, I find myself at the crossroad where this corridor meets the main one.

This is where, earlier in the day, the teacher had briefly stopped to point out directions to the toilets and the canteen. And it is then, remembering this, that I realise where the gymnasium is: it's the building I had my back to at lunchtime, with the sun, the northern sun, on my face, the canteen and playground in front of me. So it's to the south of the canteen, I think, which, when we first walked up the main corridor, the teacher told us was to our right. From where I'm standing now, then, it must be straight ahead, through that door, outside, and then presumably along a walkway or across an asphalt courtyard to—what? another wing?—and then where would the canteen be in relation to that? And then from there the gym?

I push the door open and step outside. There is a walkway, it takes me from the door, intersects another wing I've not seen before—I glimpse down dark corridors left and right—and then brings me back outside again on the other side. In front of me is the canteen, to my right the school oval, its goalposts eerie totems in the moonlight, and to my left, a little further off, a large brick building with a big sign along the wall nearest to me saying: GYMNASIUM.

It's cold outside, a chill night air, and just the faintest touch of a breeze. Though I've only been gone five minutes, I feel a long, long way away from the dinner room, the plates of food, the jugs of water, the laughter. The cold air bites my skin and I can feel my nose and upper cheeks start throbbing again. Have I come out in a bruise? And then how would I look? Look at you, she'll say, what have you got yourself mixed up in this time? I bring my fingers delicately to my face. I touch them to my nostrils then bring them up close to my eyes. It's hard to tell in this light but I can't see any blood. I walk across the dark playground to the gym. I push the door. It opens, creaks, then clicks shut behind me.

It's surprisingly light inside the gymnasium, there are big windows high on either side and through one of them I can see the moon in what now looks like a cloudless sky. The polished floor, marked out for all kinds of games in white, yellow, blue and red, reflects this moon as a very bright spot just a little way out there in front of me and the light from the windows themselves gives it all a silver sheen. But I can't see her anywhere. Suddenly I lose my nerve, for everything. If she does want to see me, if she is in here somewhere waiting for me, what will I say to her? I'm a child, truly I am, I've learned nothing so far except to do what I'm told. She is free, she has freed herself, and I am back at school. Are you there? I say. Silence. Are you there? There's a noise from the far end of the gym and then a widening vertical black line appears on the far wall. It's a door opening, a door I hadn't seen, a door opening onto a darker room beyond. In here, she says. Yes, it's her. Quick, in here, she says. I cross the gymnasium floor. She keeps the door open until I reach it then swallows me up with it.

We're in the storeroom. She stuffs an old pair of tracksuit pants in the crack under the door and turns the light on. It's a bare forty watt bulb, and against the hard fluorescent light of the dinner room the light of this forty watt bulb is warm and almost romantic. There's not much room to move: there are acrobatic mats, pieces of gym equipment, big string bags full of balls. She stands with her back to the door; I'm squeezed up between the pile of mats and the parallel bars. She looks at me; I look at her. What is this look? What happened to your face? she says. She takes a step forward, reaches out and touches my face. You're a mess, she says. In what way does she mean 'mess'? I got selected, I say. She withdraws her hand. I thought I'd never see you again, she says. They thought my story had something in it, I say, so now I'm working—and you, it's all worked out for you too. We look at each other— we know we're talking like fugitives in the storeroom of a school gymnasium: she knows, I know, we know. Sit down, she says. I sit down on one of the mats. I saw you out on the basketball court today, she says, we were pushing back the chairs, getting ready for tomorrow. We're going to take what you have written and put life into it, so Judd says anyway. *(Judd?)* He's going to run the workshop, she continues, tell us what to do, make out like he knows what he's doing. I watch her talking, pacing back and forth, all fire and passion and spontaneous voice. The other teacher will watch, she is saying, he'll nod and smile and everyone will applaud. Then they'll send us away. It's a job, Wayne, and for it we'll get dinner, a mattress on the floor and breakfast in the morning before we go. Look at me, she says, do you hear what I'm saying?

I do, sort of. But the trouble is I've not heard much since she mentioned Judd's name. A teacher? I thought he was just the factotum, the errand boy, the canteen lady. So he's been elevated to the role of teacher, he who I'd decided was my underling? And then, of course, like a twisted mind-fucking tornado-driven avalanche it hits me. Judd wasn't sent along for the ride, he's not here to serve us, he was selected as special too, selected by Polly, selected *above me*. And why was he selected? For the same reason I was selected. For the same reason all these special writers here were selected. Because we gave Polly pleasure. I look at her, still talking, her eyes alight, her face aglow. How could I? I listen to her words—it takes me a while to chase them down and catch the thread then let them pour down over me like a monsoon rain.

And so is this what we wanted? she is saying: you at school learning what you don't need to know from people unqualified to teach it; me, getting back in the Transit van tomorrow to do another corporate video, stumble my way through another humiliating audition? We don't make art, Wayne, we make money—no, we don't even do that, we live and work according to a regime invented by Andrew and those who have mentored him, a regime that says we *should* make money—submissions, proposals, tenders, budgets—but in fact we make no money, we live hand-to-mouth, use up all our energy running a so-called business and then end up coming here and doing this just so we can get a bowl of pasta. You know what we're doing tomorrow, after we've all filled up on two helpings of breakfast? We'll drive a hundred and seventy kilometres to another country town to do a used car yard ad—we're a funny circus troupe, we'll all wear funny costumes, I'll be juggling wads of money which the voice-over will tell us is the money you'll save if you take advantage of their September sale. Then back in the bus. Next day a video for the local shire about water conservation—I'm a mermaid, chroma-keyed into one of the buckets of water we're wasting. Next day a pioneer festival—everywhere a festival!—crinoline dresses and wet kisses from fat real estate agents and farm machinery salesmen.

I'm still sitting on the mat, her pacing above me, letting myself drown in her words and the shame, the utter humiliation of it all. From the moment we stepped up into the caravan, from the moment the red-lipsticked Polly ticked us off her list, we have sold it all away. What is a product anyway, what is production, productivity? Who in God's name first put the words 'arts' and 'industry' together? Who let all these bureaucrats and critics and ill-qualified pedagogues loose on the world, who gave them the right to pardon or punish? Who said we should listen? Who said we should learn, grow up? I'm off now, I can't help myself: I watch her talking, hear myself thinking, see where I am, know what I've done, feel where I want to get back to. And as I think these things, hive them off me, all this black filth, as I feel the smacks and thumps and blows, something happens—something extraordinary happens. Right before my eyes my partner changes from her thirty-something self into a thirteen-year-old other. It's like I'd set it all up. Here we are, look at us, we're back at school, we're in the storeroom at the back of the gym, the rest of the class has left for lunch; I was putting the equipment away, she's walked in and closed the door. She's in her sports uniform, a checked cotton dress. This is not some dirty fantasy, this is my partner—there she is, right there in front of me—and all the grown-up careerism has fallen from us. We are young again, both *actually* young, we are in the storeroom of the old school gymnasium and she has just locked the door. I stand up and move towards her. I've never felt like this before. I am pure innocence, naivety, and so is she. We hug, we kiss—did we ever hug or kiss like this? I move her to the pile of mats, a regal bed, and we fall together onto it. With lithe movements she unzips the dress and peels it from her. With fumbling fingers I unhook her bra. Her breasts, smooth undulations. No, they do not fall aside. I reach out a finger and touch the nipple. It does not sink, hardly gives at my touch. She is not old. What was I thinking? We are only at the threshold. We have barely even begun. She takes my hand, I come down on her. I let her arms envelop me.

four

We do not sleep, we just doze and drift for a long time in the warmth of each other's arms. When I open my eyes and look at her it feels like we've been there forever. She opens her eyes too. Let's go, I say.

It's brighter now outside, the clouds have cleared and the moon is high in the sky. It's cold, yes, but we are still basking in each other's warmth. We have no idea how long we were in there; it's all quiet, though, no-one has come looking for us; when we reach the school entrance we can see the Transit van still parked there and high up on the trees in the back corner of the schoolyard the glow from the dinner room lights. Shh, she says. We listen, and can just hear the sound of muffled voices talking, carried to us on the breeze. No-one knows we've left, no-one will miss us when we're gone: we're just another two who have fallen through the cracks. Come on, she says, I think I know where the highway is.

It must be late, because now, out on the street—a quiet suburban street of the type that you would find on the edge of any big country town—there are only one or two lights on in the houses. The sky is big, the world seems suddenly to have folded its edges back and opened itself up for us. It's very quiet. I want to giggle. I can't help myself. Shh, she says, trying not to laugh: listen. It's the sound of a truck passing, still a long way off, but clearly coming from the direction we are walking in. This way, she says. I follow her, I want always now to follow her.

There are no footpaths here, just wide grassy nature strips—there are no cars either, so we walk down the middle of the road. We pass a few streetlights before she stops again to listen. We go a little further, then turn down another street. A laundromat, a small smash repairs, a dentist's: we are getting closer to the centre of town. I feel this incredible sense of relief, of exhilaration; I don't have to work out any more what I'm supposed to do, whether what I've done is any good, whether any of it will get me anywhere or not. I come up alongside her and hold her hand. She smiles. We walk together like that, down the middle of the street, unembarrassed teenage lovers—we don't care, we'll do what we like, we'll answer to no-one, we'll tell them all to go to hell.

Another turn and we are in the main street. We walk down the footpath, past the shop windows. I wonder if anyone sees us: lovers, hand in hand. Everything is quiet, deserted. The occasional car or truck drives past, sometimes in one direction, sometimes in the other. Which way is home? I ask. She raises her finger and points in the direction we are walking. We walk to the end of town where the bright white light from an open service station makes us hold our hands up to our eyes. A couple of trucks are parked on the verge. I don't want to do it, I am a man and it will shame me, but she is full of the bravado that only actors and lunatics possess. I watch her walk inside the bright-lit restaurant. She stops and talks to a big man at one of the tables: she points outside, he looks around, first at me, then at his truck. He nods. She looks at me and gives me two thumbs up. The driver turns around again—I see him throw back his head and laugh.

Artists, says the truck driver, you don't look like artists, if I'd known that I would have left you there. We both smile, he smiles too—there is something very comforting in the knowledge that to this truck driver we don't look like artists, that we've taken him by surprise somehow, ambushed him with our ordinariness. What's wrong with artists? I ask. My partner looks sideways at me and gives me a kind of tut-tut glance.

We drive. She drifts off to sleep. I look out through the windscreen, the side window, the three-quarter moon sinking low. My eyes droop and close, when I open them we are on the outskirts of the city. The truck has pulled into a siding; a pink dawn is spreading across the sky in the east; there are rough scarred paddocks and factories around us, big half-built warehouses and machinery yards. I've got to turn here, says the truck driver, I've got to drop this load at Epping. I nudge her awake. We're here, I say. She lifts her head and rubs her eyes. You could hitch another ride, says the truck driver, or there might be a train. We'll walk, she says. We get down out of the cabin. It's cold outside and an involuntary shiver runs through me. Thanks, she says. The driver nods. Thanks, I say. I swing the door hard till it shuts. The driver revs the engine, the gears crunch, the truck drives away. We watch it slow down at the next set of lights and turn left in a slow searching arc.

We walk. We pass car yards, wrecking yards, factory outlets, warehouses. The blocks start getting smaller: retail outlets, showrooms. Now there are trees, front fences, nature strips, double-fronted houses. The sun is up, people are driving to work, listening to the serious or funny talk on the radio. The sun hits our faces, we hold our hands up and squint—it's like it's smiling at us in greeting, saying welcome home, welcome back.

We don't recognise the house at first, there's a cream and dark green picket fence out the front that was not there before. Tacked to the fence is a To Let sign. The house has been painted—cream and green. I thought they were going to demolish it? she says. Maybe just the back half, I say. We cross the front yard and step up onto the porch and with our hands cupped to the window we peer inside. The lounge room is empty. The old carpet has been ripped up and the floorboards polished. We step off the porch and walk down the driveway to the back. The shed is gone, there's a green Colourbond garage there now, at the door of which the fresh new concrete driveway ends. The plum tree, I say. It's gone. In its place a weeping cherry. The concrete yard has been dug up and relaid with a carpet of tough, almost plastic-looking grass.

All the old back half of the house is gone and has been replaced by a new extension. Big bright sunny windows and French doors open out onto the yard. We look in through the windows. Big, she says. We can see the new stove, the new benchtops, the downlights, the overhead fan. Is that the bathroom there? she asks, pointing. She pushes down on the brass-plated handle. It opens. I'm dying for a piss, she says. We go inside. Very light, very spacious. She crosses to the bathroom; I hear her pissing, a long stream.

I walk to the door that leads back into the main part of the house. It's been replastered and painted, the floors have been polished, but otherwise it's the same as before: the spare room (my 'study') first on the right, then next on the right our bedroom, opposite that the lounge room, then the front door. They just took off the back half, I think: simple, cheap.

I walk back outside. Yes, I think, it's all a façade, really; underneath it all we are still here. We never really left. I'm still sitting on the old vinyl chair out on the concrete, drinking a coffee and having my morning smoke. She's in the toilet, shouting: There's no toilet paper! Can you get me some? In this daydream I drag heavily on my cigarette and let the smoke out slowly, steadily, in a stream. I hear a plane way up, way up high in the blue: it banks towards the airport, shedding silver from its wings. The jasmine is out, and I can smell it. Wayne? she shouts. Are you there? I butt my cigarette out on the concrete, drink the last of my coffee. Soon I'll go inside to work. My work will owe nothing to no-one, except her. Then suddenly she's behind me. I used a tissue, she says.